THE WO

Nicholas Fisk has never been a worm charmer, but he has had a number of different occupations. He's served in the RAF, and been an actor in an Irish Shakespeare company, a book editor, a jazz musician, a journalist, worked in advertising and as a freelance publishing consultant. He's now a full-time author with over forty books to his credit – mainly science-fiction – and several television scripts. His books include *Backlash* (published by Walker Books), *A Rag, A Bone and A Hank of Hair* and *Time Trap*. He has also written a picture book *The Model Village* (Walker Books, 1990).

Nicholas Fisk is married with four children and lives in Hertfordshire.

"A rattling good story... It is fast, funny and totally without pretensions... Good fun."
The Sunday Times

"A good old-fashioned adventure story brought bang up to date with plenty of action, dialogue and twists and turns in the plot."
School Library Association

NICHOLAS FISK

WORM
THE
CHARMERS

WALKER BOOKS
LONDON

First published 1989 by Walker Books Ltd
87 Vauxhall Walk, London SE11 5HJ

© 1989 Nicholas Fisk

This edition published 1990

Printed in Great Britain by Cox and Wyman Ltd, Reading
Typeset in Hong Kong by Graphicraft Typesetters Ltd

British Library Cataloguing in Publication Data
Fisk, Nicholas
The worm charmers.
I. Title
823'.914   [J]
ISBN 0-7445-1448-7

Nice Worms, Good Worms

"Come up, you devils!" Shanta muttered, and tap-danced her gumbooted feet. The whites of her eyes and teeth were luminous against the rich, Indian darkness of her skin. She was in a temper.

"Oh, come *on!*" she told the worms. They did not want to hear her. They stayed in the ground. Shanta put the wooden flute to her lips and played her special worm-charming tune. She played it with great feeling. The worms took no notice.

Crump, over his shoulder, asked her, "Why don't you move away, or shut up or something?" He spoke rather crossly. He felt that Shanta was distracting his worms. But then his crumpled face – so crumpled that the eyes seemed always closed – creased into its gnome-like smile. "Another!" he said. He pulled out the worm, admiring its stretchiness, and held it up for Shanta to see. She made a rude, hooting noise through her flute. He grinned. "Can't beat the old metal rods," he told her, twanging them.

They made a vague sound as they vibrated, *Br-roomp ... pr-rroom.* The rods were a little less than his own height. He stuck them

7

about a foot into the ground then twanged them with his fingers. Worms were mad about them.

Horrie, a long way away, shouted, "How many you got, Crump?"

"Lots. More than you. Lots."

"Bet you haven't."

"Bet I have. Come and see. Bring your jar."

Horrie Horowitz, as dank and grey as the so-called summer weather, ambled over. He was eleven, about the same age as the others, but looked a hundred. His eyes were grey, his face was grey, even his blond hair was dustily greyish. "I can't imagine you as a baby," Jen had once said. She was the fourth member of the WCs, the Worm Charmers. "You must have been a sight," she said.

"I was," Horrie replied. "There's photographs. Me in my pram. Real horror-comic stuff."

Horrie had invented a special machine for worm charming. He had picked up the Acme Supersonic Vibro Miracle Clothes Washer for thirty pence at a jumble sale. You were supposed to put this thing – it looked like a small, battered spaceship – in the washing water. When you switched it on, it *vibrated* the clothes clean. It was a miracle of the New Technological Age. It did not work.

Now, converted to run off a car battery, it was employed worm charming. The battery was in a pram-wheel trolley, the Vibro Miracle was placed on the ground. When Horrie switched on, the ground trembled fizzingly. The worms, fascinated, came up to see what the fuzzy buzzing was about and Horrie put them in his jam jar.

"There you are," Horrie said. "Got more than you. Told you so."

Crump muttered, "Liar!" but it was true all the same. Horrie's jar held more worms than his. Crump said, "Bet Jen's winning, anyhow. Let's have a look at her."

The two of them turned to stare at Jen. She was using the classic worm-charming technique. She had "borrowed" her mother's expensive lightweight gardening fork. She stuck it in the ground, vibrated the handle with her fingertips and made inviting, crooning noises with her mouth. The worms loved it. They seemed to form an underground queue. At regular intervals, another worm popped its little head out of the ground. "*Good* worm," Jen said, bending down so that her long, straight golden hair brushed the victim. "*Nice* worm, *good* worm, come along then!" She seldom bothered even to pull the worm out of the ground: it just entered her jar in an orderly manner. Her jar was almost full.

Crump shivered. "Time to pack it in," he said. "Getting chilly. Back to HQ and make tea. Hot tea. Anyone coming?"

"I'm with you," Horrie said, and began packing the Vibro Miracle on its trolley. "Shanta!" he shouted. "You coming?" She shook her head violently and continued to stamp her gumboots and make horrible noises on her flute. Crump and Horrie exchanged sidelong smiles. "Driving them away," Horrie said.

They collected Jen and made for WCHQ, the barn that was their headquarters. The barn belonged to a newcomer to the village, Mr Brasen. What or whom Mr Brasen belonged to was anybody's guess. Certainly he was not part of the village. He did not belong to the land or the countryside. He had no wife or family. He was seldom seen on his own ground. He had come from nowhere in a big car, signed a big cheque and that was that. Hundred Acre Farm was his.

The barn was his too, of course – but Crump, Shanta, Horrie and Jen did not let that fact make any difference. By the law of Finders Keepers, the barn was theirs. They had always considered that they owned it, even when they were squeaky-voiced, pudgy infants. They had changed but the barn had not.

It had always been derelict and was now. Its roof, mostly of corrugated iron, showed sky through the rusty patches. Its slate tiles fell away in gangs after every storm and settled in the nettle beds. Its interior smelled of damp, rats, mould, lime, straw, fungi and creosote – an ancient can of the stuff had leaked a dark, fragrant patch, a sort of no-go area that even spiders avoided.

The barn had other attractions. There was a single window that could not be seen through because it was so grimed and cob-webbed; a tap, dangling from a sinister pipe, that let out long, wistful sighs followed by a trickle of reddish, rusty-tasting water; and a wealth of decaying harness and saddlery, vast gear wheels, shattered machinery. Also a dressmaker's dummy on a pedestal. The dummy was of a female shape not seen nowadays: a shape like a double eruption. At one time, a family of wrens had been raised in the dummy's stomach and all the babies had grown up and flown away. You don't get that sort of luck twice. All that remained was a little hole with straw sticking out of it, and the cherished memory of the baby wrens.

In short, the barn had always been part of the WCs' lives; and if Mr Brasen wanted them out, bad luck Mr Brasen.

Crump filled the WCs' black-bottomed aluminium kettle from the tap, pumped up the ancient Primus, primed it with meths and set fire to it. When it had gone through its usual blue-flames and yellow-flames-with-choking-smoke stages and settled down to producing

11

a coronet of blue flames, he made real tea with real milk and lots of sugar. The WCs did not fool around with powdered milk and tea bags.

"Supercolossal," Jen said as the tea burned her lips.

"Nice brew," Horrie said, raising his mug to Crump.

Shanta came in looking cross. "Well, I got three, anyhow," she said disgustedly, holding up her jar. "All that effort for just three mouldy worms... I've got mud on the ends of my hair, just look. Ah, *tea*..."

She cupped her thin brown fingers round her mug and sat crosslegged. Crump watched her drink, thinking: She's got style, old Shanta. He liked the long curve of her nose, the dark glitter of her eyes, her narrow yet not skinny hands and limbs, her blacker-than-black long hair.

Everyone drank tea. Nobody spoke. The WCs spent a lot of time not talking. They knew each others' thoughts. So when Jen finished her first mugful and said, "Anyone seen him?" everyone knew who she meant: Mr Brasen, of course.

"He won't be round," Crump said. "Too damp and chilly for him. He'll be in the farmhouse, if he's here at all, doing his – doing his..."

"Doing what?" Shanta said. "Just what

12

does he do?"

Crump shrugged.

Horrie said to Shanta, "If anyone knew anything about him, you would, wouldn't you?" He was referring to the General Store, the most important place in the village. Shanta's parents ran it; which meant that they could hardly avoid knowing about other people's affairs – what their hobbies and interests were (from the newspapers and magazines they ordered), what they ate and drank, how promptly they paid their bills, how many letters they posted or got each week (for the General Store was also a Sub Post Office).

"Go on, Shanta," Jen said, "tell us about Mr Brasen."

It was Shanta's turn to shrug. No one was surprised at her refusal to talk. Shanta and her parents were not gossip-mongers – that was one of the many things the village liked about them. When the Patels had first arrived, they were greeted with stares, cold shoulders and the occasional muttered nastiness ("Don't need any of their sort here!"). Then two things happened. . .

For the first time in living memory, the General Store sold good goods – cheese that wasn't sweating and cracked, rashers that hadn't turned to leather. You even got the right newspapers delivered early. That was Shanta on her bike.

Second, there was Ma Hoskings. Her only neighbours were the Patels. Everyone clicked their tongues about Ma Hoskings: the poor old thing, nobody to look after her, she won't last out another winter. Then the great snow came, and the flu – everyone caught it, even the District Nurse. It was Mrs Patel who nursed Ma Hoskings and kept her fire going; Mr Patel who battled his way through the snowdrifts to get her to the County Hospital when she surrendered at last to the flu.

"I'm not a-dying," Ma Hoskings announced from her hospital deathbed, "until Mrs Patel comes to see me off proper." Mrs Patel came. Ma Hoskings died, with a hand to hold. And the District Nurse made sure that the village heard about it. From then on, the Patels quietly assumed their rightful place in the village.

"Oh, go on, Shanta!" Jen insisted. "Mr Brasen: you must know *something* about him . . ."

"Leave her alone," Crump said. "Mind your own business. Anyhow, I've told you: he won't be round to bother us."

There were squelching footsteps outside, the deep bark of a big dog, a shadow that became a shape filling the door of the barn – and there he was. Mr Brasen.

O – U – T. Out!

"I want you out," he said. "Sorry, but there it is. O – U – T. Out!"

Mr Brasen's Alsatian dog wagged its tail twice, lowered its head and showed its teeth nastily at each of the WCs in turn. Mr Brasen showed his teeth too. He smiled.

He had good teeth and his smile should have been reassuring. Somehow it was not. It came and went too quickly. It was too small and square.

"That stove of yours," he said, nodding at the flickering old Primus, "that's a fire risk. And there's legal complications. You wouldn't understand, but what it amounts to is, I want you out. As of now."

"It's our barn!" Crump said indistinctly.

"Not so, sonny," said Mr Brasen. Crump flinched at the "sonny". "My land, my barn. O – U – T. Out! If you please!"

The WCs stared blankly at him, taking in the square shoulders, the square smile, the slab-sided cheeks like newly-cut ox tongue, the sharply barbered hair under the new-looking check cap. He was dressed as a countryman, yet looked a townic.

"Our things," Jen said, indicating them with a nervous sweep of her arm.

"Take them with you," said Mr Brasen.

"Take them now."

"But we've always had the barn —"

"Out you go," said Mr Brasen flatly. The dog's head dropped still lower and its tongue slithered over its teeth.

Five minutes later, they were walking away from the barn carrying the Primus, the kettle, the mugs, the rat-nibbled WC library of bashed paperbacks and a hundred other possessions, all priceless. Mr Brasen's eyes followed the slow, melancholy procession. His dog watched too.

Jen waited till dusk and distance hid her from Mr Brasen before she began to cry. "After all those years..." she said. "How could he?"

"He could. He did," Crump said, grimly. "So what's the good of snivelling? You too, Shanta." For Shanta was also dripping tears from the end of her finely curved nose.

Horrie suddenly said, "Wait!" and stopped walking.

"Well?" said the others.

"That was his Land Rover," Horrie said. "Didn't you hear it? So he's gone!"

"So what?"

"Well, when do you think he'll be coming back?"

"Some time. Any time. Who knows?"

"Well, I'm going back now!" Horrie told them. "I'm going to dump all this stuff back

16

in the barn – find hiding places for everything, so we can take things out when we need them, whenever we feel like it. He's not chucking *me* out of my HQ!" He marched off without a backward look.

The three remaining WCs stared after him – looked at each other – and silently followed Horrie, trudging muddily through the gloom.

"We ... shall ... we shall not be moved!" Jen sang, quietly.

In the barn they relit the Primus and squatted on their heels to drink tea by the stove's jumpy light, mostly blue, sometimes yellow.

"Down with Brasen!" Crump said. The WCs clinked mugs and grinned.

"A toast!" Horrie said. "A toast to us – the WCs!" They clinked again.

"If old Brasen wants us out," Horrie said, "he'll have to flush us out. Flush, get it? Flush the WCs! Clever joke, ho, ho, ho."

It felt so good to be back in the barn that the others actually laughed.

Brasen's Worms

They became bored with worm charming. In their time, the WCs had been the Blood Brotherhood, the Secret Four, the Angels of Mercy and half a dozen other grand and glorious things. Once, for a whole week, they had turned into Robot Invaders and moved in jerks. You got a stiff neck doing it. Each phase had lost its appeal, become kid-stuff or old-hat or boring. Now worm charming was almost over.

Worm charming became interesting again because of Mr Brasen, of all people. On that particular day, the WCs were trying to do wheelies round the war memorial on their bikes. Only Crump was any good at wheelies. He had cannibalized a junior bike with fat-tyred wheels, ape-hanger bars and a lot of silver tape and purple paint. The result looked awful but sometimes did wheelies.

Mr Brasen's Land Rover suddenly appeared, slowed and stopped. Mr Brasen's head poked out of the door. He said, "You want to make some money?"

He could not have chosen a better opening remark. The WCs never had any money. Jen was the only one with rich parents, but their religion was horses and Jen hated anything on hooves. When Jen asked for money, her parents cried, "But what *for?*" As Jen could never reply with anything horsy, she seldom received more than the odd 50p. "I'm not horsy, so they keep me on a short rein. Ho, ho, ho."

Shanta earned money the hard way, by doing her paper round. She knew – her parents did not – that she was under-paid. Like Jen, she reckoned her fortune in pennies. But it never occurred to Shanta to ask for more.

Crump had no money because he was generous. Given a pound (and he seldom was) he cried, "Let's celebrate!" and lashed out on colas and crisps for everyone. Had he won the pools, everyone would have received Rolls-Royces and Ferraris.

Horrie never had any money because he was a collector. His most lasting craze was old typewriters. He advertised for old typewriters in shop windows and already owned a Blickendörfer, a Bar-Lock, a birdcage Oliver, an Empire portable – and a Mignon! A Mignon! A two-key, interchangeable-head, stylus-operated Mignon! These machines needed constant attention and money if they were to be kept alive – typewriter ribbons, solder, small tools and all the rest of it. They even demanded blood. Horrie's fingers were constantly scarred by typewriter mechanisms that fought back. Horrie never had any money.

"You want to make some money?" Mr

Brasen called, and instantly had the full attention of the WCs.

"We do," Crump replied. "How much? What for?"

"We'll do anything for money," Jen said, dreamily. "Anything."

"It needn't be legal," Horrie pointed out.

"They tell me you charm worms," Mr Brasen said. "Is that right?"

"I'm best at it," Crump lied. "It's me you need. You really *have* got worms?"

"My lawn has," Mr Brasen said. "Wormcasts everywhere. Chemicals don't work. I'll give you money to catch the worms."

"We're rather expensive," Shanta said, her dark eyes calculatingly slanted. "Professional services. So much a jar."

"*How* much a jar?" said Mr Brasen.

"Fifty pence," Jen said. Her voice betrayed her. She sounded unsure.

Mr Brasen said, "Nonsense. I'll give you twenty. Take it or leave it."

"We'll take it!" Shanta said instantly.

Mr Brasen said, "Hm. You're sure you can really charm worms? I'm serious about this. That lawn is supposed to be a showpiece and I want to keep it that way."

"Twenty pence a jar," Horrie said. "How can you lose? Either we charm worms or we don't. You'll see the results – glass jars are transparent. Hundreds of worms. Thousands of worms."

"I'll show you worms!" Crump said, vain-gloriously.

"All right then. Agreed," said Mr Brasen. "I want you to go to work on Friday."

"Friday?" said the WCs, all at once. "But that's four days away! We want to get started now! We need the money now!"

"Friday afternoon or not at all. One o'clock sharp, on Friday. Well?"

"All right, Friday," Crump muttered.

"We would consider accepting a deposit. An advance. A down-payment," Shanta said, loftily. She knew these terms from helping with the General Store. They sounded impressive.

Mr Brasen was not impressed. "Friday, one o'clock, prompt!" was all he said as he drove off.

On Wednesday, it rained heavily. On Thursday, it rained during the afternoon, gently.

"Perfect!" Crump said.

"Ideal!" Jen beamed.

"Bring out worms like daffodils in spring!" Horrie said.

"Here you are," Shanta said. "Catch hold. Your jam jars. Two each. We'll be lucky to fill half that number, but you never know. Just think: six jars at twenty pence ... "

"One pound twenty!" muttered Jen, wrapping her arms round herself to hug herself. But then she became businesslike. "I saw a Western the other night," she said. "A Western on telly. Cowboys. It was all about gold prospecting. Some cowboys put all their money into buying the deeds of a gold mine, but the baddies had been there first and it turned out that the mine had been salted. Wasn't that sad?"

She looked very dreamy and spiritual – almost angelic – with the sun lighting her golden hair. The other WCs were immediately suspicious.

"You're up to something!" Shanta accused. "Anyhow – what do you mean, 'salted'?"

"Well, the baddies – the people who sold the poor cowboys the mine – got some nuggets of gold and sprinkled them around in the mine to make it seem there was lots of gold. But of course there wasn't any. So the cowboys lost their all. It really was sad."

"*So...?*" Shanta said.

"What's it got to do with us?" Horrie demanded.

"I was just wondering," Jen said, looking more saintly than ever, "just wondering if a person could salt a *lawn*. Just wondering."

"Salt a lawn?" Crump said.

"With worms," Jen said. "I mean, we've got till Friday. Suppose we did a little worm charming in advance: *now,* for instance. Sup-

22

pose we got lots of worms, jam jars full...
Well, on Friday, we'd have a head start,
wouldn't we?"

"But that would be cheating!" Shanta said.
"He wants *his* worms caught!"

"Well, he's cheated us!" Jen said, suddenly
not looking saintly at all. "He's cheated us
out of our HQ! Thrown us out! Cheek! So
why shouldn't we get our own back?"

"No!" Horrie said.

"No!" said Shanta, firmly.

"No!" said Crump, reluctantly.

"Oh, well," Jen said, brushing back her
sunlit, golden hair, "it was just a thought."

On Friday, at one o'clock precisely, the WCs
arrived at Mr Brasen's.

They were fully prepared to make money.
Shanta now had two flutes stuck together
with sticky tape instead of a single flute.
"Sympathetic harmonics," she explained.
"Good vibes."

Horrie had modified the Acme Supersonic
Vibro Miracle. Now the rods that stuck out
of the spaceship body carried two cracked
billiard-balls, one red and one white. These,
he explained, would vibrate in sympathy with
the Vibro Miracle and produce cross-currents
that would drive the worms mad with curiosity.

Jen had polished her mother's long-handled

23

fork and was already murmuring, "*Good* worms! Come along, then! *Nice* worms!" as she looked for the ideal site.

Crump, severe and determined, had done nothing to his simple steel rods. But he was first to get his equipment set up. He frowned as he probed and prodded, looking for the best place. The choice was enormous because the lawn was enormous.

"It's funny," he said to Jen as he stuck in his final rod, "I don't see any wormcasts. Mr Brasen said the lawn was being ruined by casts. Well, where are they?"

Jen was about to answer – she too was puzzled – when Shanta struck up on her twin flutes. The noise was horrible, like two piglets having their tails twisted simultaneously. Jen rolled her eyes and took her fork elsewhere.

Horrie connected the car battery to the modified Vibro Miracle. There were blue sparks, a spitting sound – and Horrie danced about with his hands clenched in his armpits, his ashen hair standing straight up. Crump grinned wickedly and called out, "Trying the old dancing routine, then, Horrie? Given up electronics?" He began his gumboot dance.

Horrie swore, licked his burned fingers and once again bent over the Vibro Miracle. This time there was no trouble. The Vibro vibed, the billiard-balls trembled on their stalks. Horrie lay down on the grass beside his machine, hands behind his head. "You do the dancing," he told Crump. "A real disco dolly, you are. Top of the flops."

The sun came in and out of the big fluffy white clouds. Minutes and hours passed. Crump's gingery face reddened with the effort of dancing and thrumming, but he kept at it. Shanta, tired of complaints from the others, fluted hideously from a remote corner of the great lawn. "I've got one, I've got a worm!" she shouted.

"It's probably tone deaf," Crump murmured.

At three-thirty, they downed tools, drank colas and compared results. Results were poor. Horrie had filled one jam jar, Jen almost one, Crump almost one — and Shanta had managed exactly seven worms. She was fed up. "They taste revolting after a while, these flutes," she said. "And they get sort of smelly, too."

"All your germs," Crump told her. "Festering away round the flute holes. Breeding like flies."

"Oh, do shut up. Give me my cola."

"I wouldn't drink it, if I were you," Horrie told Shanta. "Sweet things are what germs like best . . . especially when they're wriggling and breeding."

"Oh, *shut up*."

"I'll drink it for you if you like," Horrie

25

offered. "Save you from a horrible death." But Shanta forced herself to finish her cola, just to spite him.

"I still don't get it," Crump said. "He said there were worms. Too many worms. And we've the right weather and everything – but where are they? Why aren't we getting millions of worms?"

"Because we're sitting here yacking instead of worm charming," Horrie said. He got to his feet and returned to the Vibro Miracle. The others followed.

Horrie had the easiest time of it. He had merely to sit or lie by his machine. The others had to do real work while he looked about him and thought thoughts. It really was strange, he thought, that there were no wormcasts; Crump was right. It was almost as if Mr Brasen had been telling them a pack of lies. But why should he bother to lie about worms and wormcasts?

It would be stupid to invent lies about things like that ... and Mr Brasen did not seem a stupid man. Not stupid at all. Tough rather than stupid. Big, slabby, tough. You have to be tough, Horrie thought, to have made the money to buy the farm and the farmhouse and all this – and then not even use the place, or enjoy it. You have to be tough not to notice the coldness of the people in the village. Even the way he drove his Land

Rover was tough: slam in the gears, bang the door, slap on the brakes. Tough, tough, tough.

Tuff-tuff-tuff, echoed the Vibro Miracle, as it blurred and blithered away on its patch of grass. Horrie noticed two worm heads breaking surface and forgot about Mr Brasen.

At four-thirty, the WCs began to flag. Jen was doing well – she had filled one jam jar – but was bored. Crump had done even better and was chanting a song that went, "Put your head in a basin, Mr Brasen." Jen could tell that he was play-acting to keep himself amused. Horrie, with two jars half filled, now rested on his stomach eating grass.

Shanta was in the doldrums. "They've gone all soggy!" she shouted, holding up her flutes. "The mouthpieces have gone all squishy, I can't play the tunes any more, I mean it's hopeless!" No one offered her sympathy. "I've had enough!" she shouted. "I'm sick of it all! Why don't we stop?"

But then Jen shouted, "Three! All at once!" – and Horrie was fiddling with the Vibro Miracle – and Crump was moving his rods to fresh ground – and nobody took any notice of Shanta. So she gathered her things together and marched off, without a word.

A few minutes later, Horrie shouted, "Hey! Where's Shanta gone?"

Crump said, "Dunno. She wasn't getting any worms, not like me – I'm doing fine. Come and look!"

In fact, he was doing badly. He and Jen started to argue about who had most. The shadows lengthened on the great lawn.

The three continued for another half-hour or more, then it began to rain, hard. "And we call it *summer*!" Crump said. "Pack it in, right? We'll collect old Shanta and go to the barn and make tea. I wonder where she is?"

"She'll have gone home to the General Store," Horrie said. "Either that or WCHQ. Let's try the store first and buy some crisps. I'm starving."

They went to the General Store. Shanta was not there. Jen said, "She'll be at HQ, we'll go there next. Can we leave our worms here, Mrs Patel?" Mrs Patel pulled a face but laughed her easy laugh and said, "Yes. And will you tell Shanta she must be home before seven, it is most important, she is cooking the dinner and she must take some things out of the oven at seven precisely or I will be most cross." Again she laughed, but the WCs knew that she meant what she said. The Patels were a disciplined family.

By now the rain had stopped and the time was 5.45. It took nearly a quarter of an hour to walk to the barn. There was no Shanta. Crump said, "Well ... let's brew up anyhow.

She'll turn up. I mean, where else would she go?"

They brewed up. Shanta did not arrive.

At 6.40, they were ready to leave WCHQ. Jen said, "I wish Shanta had come. It's odd."

Horrie said, "She's probably sulking at home. Because she didn't get any worms."

Jen said, "But Shanta doesn't sulk," which was true.

Crump said, "She'll be at home, you see."

They had entered the barn by their new, secret way – a hole near the back, in a side wall. They left, however, from the front. Even if Mr Brasen had been looking for them to come or go, he would not have seen them. The sky was almost black with cloud. It was getting dark. But not so dark that they could fail to see the tracks when Crump stumbled in one of them.

They stooped to examine them. Tyre tracks, lots of them.

"Land Rover," Horrie said, digging his toe into one pattern in the mud. "Probably Mr Brasen."

"But what about these, the ones that tripped me?" Crump said, pointing to much deeper, wider tracks, some of them skidmarks. "Something heavy," he said, "with big rear wheels. A lorry. Who'd want to bring a lorry here?"

Horrie said, "Look: car." He pointed to yet

another set of tracks. "Michelin GX or what-ever it is," he said. "Medium or big car. I suppose they could have been there before but we never noticed…"

"No," said Jen. "They're all new. If they weren't, they wouldn't be so clear after all that rain."

Horrie said, "Well, there you are. Does it matter?"

Jen and Crump thought for a moment and then, both at once, said, "Suppose not."

Then Horrie said, "We'll just call in at the General Store on our way home, OK?"

They called in. It was well after seven and Shanta was not there and had not been there. Mrs Patel's warm brown skin had gone a dirty colour. She kept saying, "It is not like her."

Mr Patel said, "Now I really will telephone the police, I really will." And did so.

He talked for a long time on the telephone, constantly rubbing his forehead and eyes with a hand that shook.

Calamity

Shanta kept licking her lips as she walked away from Mr Brasen's house. She was trying to get rid of the taste of the flutes. "Stupid worms!" she muttered; then "Ugh ... ugh ..." She wanted to spit to clean out her mouth and cautiously looked about her in the gathering darkness to make sure she was alone. She was. "Pooh ... pooh ... pooh!" she went, but the taste of the flutes' mouthpieces still lingered.

Suddenly furious, she tore the two flutes apart and flung them up into the hedge. They were only junky little things, anyhow. Her parents sold them for fifteen pence each or four for fifty pence.

She walked on, feeling her bad temper dissolve as the air became fresher and chillier against her cheeks and brow. A sudden loud, crackling, snorting noise from behind the hedge startled her; a trampling, rushing sound frightened her. Then she laughed aloud and said, "Calamity Jane!"

The pony snorted in reply. Calamity Jane belonged to a girl called Anne Clough, a small plump girl with a face like a cheerful marmalade pudding. When Shanta was past the high part of the hedge, Calamity Jane became visible, pounding along tossing her mane, then

31

stopping to be talked to. "We went worm charming today, Calamity – don't pull your head back like that! – and I came last." The pony's large, beautiful eyes looked deeply sympathetic. "I'm glad you're sorry for me, you nice thing!" Shanta told the pony. She walked on, stopping more than once because Calamity Jane expected it.

Shanta was making for the barn. She knew the others would end up at WCHQ because tea-making was a sort of ceremony. When you finished doing something, you went to HQ and made tea. After tea, she would go home: she had to be home before seven because it was her turn to cook, her father's turn to serve and her mother's turn to lay the table. Her father was by far the best cook. Shanta had a sudden mental snapshot of him, with the big spoon to his mouth, tasting what he had prepared with a sort of mystical look on his face. She smiled and only half heard the sound of engines. The sound came from the barn.

She crawled under a familiar fence wire, put her foot on a familiar stepping-stone, held out her right hand to grasp the familiar branch that kept you balanced as you stepped over the hedge by the barn – and froze.

In front of the barn was Mr Brasen's Land Rover, a BMW saloon and an olive-green lorry like an army truck.

And then there was a man – he came from nowhere – behind her.

The man said, "All right, girlie," and grabbed her. His right hand curled itself into her long black hair and yanked her head back; his left clamped over her mouth to silence her scream. She felt the hard pads of skin on the palm of his hand against her lips and smelled the cigarette smell of his fingers.

The man said, "Flippin' hedge... Right, you keep going forward and I go with you. Nice and easy, now." They got through the hedge still locked together. He said, "You make a noise and I'll pull your head off your shoulders, right?" Then he took his left hand away from her mouth, seized her left arm and forced it up between her shoulder blades. She cried out without meaning to because he hurt her.

Again, he jerked her head back by the hair and said, "Quiet or I'll *hurt* you." She did not make a sound. She knew he would do what he threatened simply by the tone of his voice.

When they were free of the hedge and in the field leading to the barn, he said, "Open your mouth." She obeyed. He said, "Wider!" Suddenly her mouth was filled with cloth – his handkerchief it must have been – that smelled of cigarettes. Her knees felt so weak that she stumbled as he pushed her on. The man grunted and hit her in the small of the back with his fist. "Straighten up," he said. "Keep walking."

They were at the barn. She fell to her knees in mud. There were several men doing things; she could not make it all out. Carrying things, loading things. They were in a hurry, not talking much. "No, that one goes over there." "Move it, move it!" – things like that. Shanta felt sick. The handkerchief was choking her, she wanted to go home. Home by seven at the latest to cook dinner.

She thought she saw Mr Brasen but perhaps she did not. A man in a quilted anorak seized her by the jaw. His hard fingers dug in. His angry eyes glared into hers. "What we got here, then? Just what we don't need!" He and the man who had captured her were arguing. The glaring man said, "Why didn't you just knock her cold and leave her?" Mumbled reply. "Well, what're we going to do with her now? That's what I want to know!" Another mumble. "What do you mean, take her with us? And then what?"

Shanta stared dumbly, looking from one towering shape to the other, trying to remember faces, make her brain work. But she was trembling and her eyes watered because the man had pulled her hair so hard and she was afraid.

Then Mr Brasen was there, staring down at her. He was angry with her, angry with the men. It was *his* hand that clutched her hair now and dragged and pulled and rushed her to the lorry and heaved her over its tailgate into the interior. She fell sprawling on the metal floor and there was a noise, the self-starter grinding, then the engine caught and the floor shook and heaved and lurched: they were going. A man's hands came from the blackness and fumbled at her, grabbing her. His voice said, "All right, all right, calm down!" as if she were struggling, but she wasn't, it was just that she was pulling the gag out of her mouth and also being thrown about on the floor of the lorry as it went over the rough ground.

There was a final lurch and heave as the lorry left the broken ground and reached tarmac. Now it was accelerating along the road with its gears yowling and grinding.

She managed at last to steady herself and settle on her hands and knees. The man's hands were still on her, one gripping her hair and the other awkwardly clamped on her shoulder, not very hard, as if he too were embarrassed by the stupidity and untidiness of it all.

"Let go of me!" she shouted. He more or less let her go. Now he held her only by the upper arm. "Look," he said, "you don't want to —"

"You don't treat girls like that!" she shouted, furiously. Then, to her own surprise and disgust, she started crying, loudly.

She stopped crying and looked about her. There was little to see. The man. Two other men, squatting some distance away near the cabin and driver. Small plywood packing cases, several cartons with the cover of one package stuck on each carton to identify the contents. The trademark was a red cross in a blue shield. Medical supplies, Shanta thought.

The man said, "Got a hold of yourself, then?" She nodded. "No use making a fuss," he said. "I mean, you're in it now, like it or not."

"What am I in?" she demanded. "What are you doing with me?" She thought of home and getting the dinner and the WCs and the real things, and wanted to cry again. But what good would that do?

Think! She told herself.

This man sitting above her, holding her arm: who was he? And what? Nobody important, she decided. Not important or clever. Not one of the bosses. Not somone like Mr Brasen.

And the two other men: they just sat there, hunched, doing nothing and saying nothing.

Not important either.

"You're hurting my arm!" she told the man above her. "Let go!" That was a mistake. His grip tightened. "*Please* let me go!" she said, looking up at him, knowing that her eyes would look big and dark and soft, wondering if he would respond. He did. He let her arm go. "But I'm keeping hold of your hair, right?" he said. He held the ends of her hair, not pulling at them. "Thank you!" she said, demurely, and went on thinking.

She had plenty of time to think. The lorry went on, noisily and grumblingly. How long had she been inside it? How fast were they going? Where were they? We must have done at least twenty miles, she thought. And it's so dark. And as we haven't passed through any villages or towns, we're not on the Bellminster main road. But are we heading north, south, east or west?

Sometimes cars passed them. One screamed past, two-tone horns blaring. Probably a sports car, young man with his girlfriend. Shanta thought, when I'm grown up, I'll have a boyfriend with a sports car. I'll do my hair with a red Alice band and wear a white dress with white shoes and a red sash. And red nails.

Oh, come on! she told herself. *Think!*

Sometimes the lorry's engine or gearbox made a funny noise. It went *Yerrk!* She waited

for the sound. Ah, there it was – *Yerr-errk!*
Could the noise be useful?

She decided it could. Next time the noise
came, she looked up at the man and said,
"Your friend over there is going to be sick."

"Don't be daft!" the man said. Then he
called out, "You all right, Clyde?" (Clyde!
Shanta thought. Remember that!)

"All right?" Clyde shouted back. "Why
shouldn't I be?"

"Perhaps it was the other man," Shanta
suggested. "Not Clyde. Harry!" She had invented the name.

"Harry?" her man said. "That's not Harry!
I'm Harry. That's *Dave*!" Shanta silently repeated the names she had learned. To herself,
she said, Harry: shortish, broad, dark, wearing donkey jacket. Clyde: green anorak, big
shoes, square face, brown hair. Dave: lanky,
dark blue jacket with flapped pockets, can't
see his hair. Harry, Clyde, Dave.

The lorry again made its noise. *Yerrk.*

"It's Dave that's going to be sick," Shanta
told her man. "Just look at him. You can tell
he's not well!"

Harry looked over at Dave, who was hunched in the corner. He swayed when the lorry
swayed. He *could* have been ill... "Don't
know what you're on about," Harry said,
uncertainly. "Hey, Dave! You OK?"

Dave said, "What d'you mean?" and

looked puzzled.

The lorry went, *Yerrk*. It did it when the driver changed down a gear, Shanta now knew. The driver had just changed down because they were coming to road works. There were red lanterns going by and posts with strips of reflective stuff like ribbons. The lorry was going slower as the road narrowed. Shanta pretended to scratch her head and neck. She scratched hard to give Harry time to get used to the position of her hand. She changed its position very slightly so that she could grasp her own hair close to the skull with all four fingers. Harry, worried about Dave, seemed not to notice. Now his hand grasped only the ends of her hair.

The lorry *yerrked* and slowed still more.

Shanta jerked her hair out of Harry's hand – got both her own hands on the tailboard – flexed her legs – and vaulted.

The Forest

She hit the road in a rolling mess of hurting knees, elbows and ankles. Even as she landed, she heard Harry shouting and saw his leg swing over the tailgate. The lorry ground on – there were shouts – the lorry braked – Harry half jumped and half fell out of the back. Shanta tripped over the reflective tapes and fell in a ditch. Harry was shouting, "My ankle! My ankle!" Shanta had time to hope it hurt. Then she got up and started running.

She ran into a confusion of ferns, bushes and forest. She ran furiously at first. As the forest thickened around her, she slowed down and looked over her shoulder. She saw the roadwork lanterns and the lorry's tail lamps, both red; and the yellowish fans of light from the headlamps, against which were silhouetted the shapes of men running towards her. One man had a torch.

Shanta kept running until she found what she wanted: a small clearing. She scrabbled in the pockets of her jeans, found a comb and handkerchief and dropped them both. She remembered her plastic bracelets. She pulled off two, snapped them in half and threw the pieces on the ground. She threw more pieces straight ahead of her. All these bright things showed up well. They made a rough line leading back to the men.

She turned sharp right and ran deep into the forest.

She found the right tree – an old, untidy oak with some low, sagging branches. To Shanta, climbing such a tree was like climbing stairs.

Near the top of the tree, she made herself comfortable in a V of branches and willed the men to keep coming along the path she had first taken, the straight line from the road. They did as she willed and discovered the clues she had deliberately planted. She heard Harry shout, "Straight on, then!" and even glimpsed the light of the torch as they clumped ahead, earnestly going in the wrong direction.

Shanta waited and watched. She knew what would happen. The men would grow tired. So would their torch battery. They'd argue, quarrel and stumble back to the lorry. She only had to wait.

And there they were, voices loud, footsteps uncertain; and there they went, the lorry grinding its gears and making its noises; and she was alone.

She climbed down the tree and collected her comb and handkerchief. Her nose was running, it was quite cold, but the moon often showed through the clouds, it was not going to rain. She blew her nose, combed her hair and began walking.

When she reached the road, she waited for a breeze then threw her handkerchief in the air. It floated to the left, the direction the lorry had taken. Very well, then. She would walk in that direction. She rubbed her elbows as she walked. They were bruised from her escape. Her left knee hurt quite a lot too.

Apart from these annoyances, her mind was calm. It was not her fault that she had missed cooking dinner. She was not afraid of being alone in the dark. She was sorry for her parents' anxiety but that would soon be over.

Meanwhile, she just had to keep walking.

The Glint

In the General Store, PC Thurston said, "I'm very sorry, Mrs Patel, I wish there was more I could do. But I've got on to Division. There'll be an Incident car coming any minute now ..." He looked yet again at his big wristwatch. "Any minute now," he said.

Jen, Horrie and Crump were there. Jen had taken the dinner out of the oven when Mrs Patel's back was turned. It was a charred mess, of course. Mrs Patel and her husband had not even noticed the smell of burning. Jen went to Mrs Patel and put her thin arm round the woman's plump shoulder. "You are a nice girl, a nice girl," Mrs Patel said weakly. Tears ran down her cheeks. She had long ago stopped wiping them away. "But are you all sure there is no more to tell?"

Horrie said, "Honest, there's nothing. Nothing. She finished first and went off on her own and we got on with the worm charming for another half-hour or so and then..."

"And there was no quarrelling? No upset?" Mrs Patel said.

"No, nothing like that at all. Shanta was just bored with it, not angry or anything. We'd tell if there'd been anything."

"It is so," said Mr Patel, pausing for a moment from his endless walking up and down. "You are good friends, we know that. Like family. It is not you, it is something else, someone else." His face was the colour of putty and shining with sweat that was not sweat.

PC Thurston said, "I'll go out and have another look round if you like. On my bike. But Divsion's coming any minute..." He was a big, pink man, too kind ever to become used to the troubles of others.

Crump could not stand any more of it. "*I'm* going," he said. "Just bike around. I might see something, I've got a dynamo..." He meant, we've worn out a dozen torch batteries and found nothing but I must look again.

He cycled into the darkness, standing on the pedals to get up speed. He wanted action, speed, anything that would blanket the sick feeling in his throat and stomach. Pedalling hard made his dynamo produce brighter light. The lamp gave a good beam, a narrow spot surrounded by a big halo. As he rode, he waved hello to Mr and Mrs Bonnard, on their way to the General Store. He wondered how they had got the news and how many more neighbours would crowd into that little room and what good anyone could do.

He rode to Mr Brasen's house, then turned round and came back, following the route that Shanta must have taken. He made stops

44

and detours, searching driveways, alleys, fences, the gated entrances to fields. The moon helped when the dynamo could not. He even looked behind the greenhouse in Mr Bonnard's garden, feeling a fool as he did so.

Now he rode by the big, loose hedge flanking one side of the road leading to the barn. It was all so familiar that he found it hard to concentrate. He had to force himself to use his eyes. Calamity Jane wickered at him and thumped alongside parallel to him on the other side of the hedge. The pony wanted him to stop and chat. Another time, Calamity Jane.

Something glinted high up in the hedge. What was it? Whatever it was it could have nothing to do with Shanta. She was hardly likely to be perched halfway up a hedge.

But again, something glinted in the hedge. Crump stopped his bike, lifted the rear wheel and pedalled to keep the dynamo going while he angled his headlamp to pick up the glinting thing.

It was nothing but a piece of shiny brown wood.

He sighed, mounted his bike and rode on – then braked sharply. Hedges don't have shiny pieces of wood in them.

He turned back, found the place and spotlighted it. His mouth pursed as if to whistle but no sound came out.

The shiny bit of wood was one of Shanta's two flutes, the flutes she had stuck together. He could see a tongue of sticky tape dangling.

He backtracked further and found the other flute.

Then he pedalled like mad to the General Store, where blue and white Police Rovers were parked, their blue lamps flashing as they revolved.

Butterfly and Pollitt

Now Crump was in a Police Rover with a uniformed driver called Pete, a bony, plain-clothes detective and a uniformed police-woman apparently called Butterfly. Later, he learned that she was called WPC Butterfield.

They seemed not to speak English. Every-thing was in a muttered code. The driver would say something like, "Yeah, PRX on BCD," into a little handset that squeaked at him from the dash when it wanted his atten-tion. Then he might say, "Oh... thuh-ree...fife on MCP," which would shut up the handset for a few minutes.

Butterfly prevented Crump from breaking the code by asking him questions. "About Shanta, now," she said in Crump's ear. "What was she wearing?"

"Sort of denims," Crump said. "And those lightweight green gumboots, half-length, you know."

"Merriboots, would that be what she was wearing?"

"Yes. Merriboots. Green."

"What colour denims, now?"

"Blue. No, wait! They were red. I'm sure they were red."

"And her top. What sort of a top, now?"

Crump's lips moved but no words came

out. He was bitterly ashamed of himself. He realized that he simply did not know what Shanta had been wearing. Had it been a sweater, an anorak, or what? Yet his mind was filled with pictures of Shanta. Shanta snowballing in her father's duffle coat, much too big for her; Shanta in a striped T-shirt that day she fell in the stream; Shanta in a sort of yellow party frock at the fête, looking smashing. And a fat lot of good all *that* was, if he couldn't remember what she wore this very day.

"Ah, well," Butterfly said. "What about that photograph in her home, now? Is it recent? Would she still be wearing her hair in that style?" Instead of answering these questions, Crump's mind asked stupid questions of its own, such as, where does Butterfly come from? Is that a Northern Irish accent?

But suddenly, just as they neared the flutes in the hedge, his mind jumped into the right gear. He said, "I've got it! She was wearing a yellow T-shirt, a sort of cotton thing! And she'd a grey what-d'you-call-it – a blouson – a big one, she wore it like a sack over her back with the sleeves tied in front! And —"

"We're there, aren't we?" said the detective. The Rover stopped. "Now, you just lead us to the very spot. The spot itself. Have a torch."

Crump swung the big torch and said,

"There!"

"Right, up on my shoulders. Take off your boots first, I don't want suspicious footprints all over me. Right, up you go…"

They recovered both flutes. The detective studied them. "Why up there in the hedge? Don't answer me. Because she was fed up with them and chucked them away. Because she hadn't caught any worms. Right? Right. Where did she go after that? She went the way she always went. Now, you show us that way. Lead on, Macduff."

Crump led them through a gate and into a field. It was like a film. Blue-grey darkness, the beams of the torches swinging and jittering, figures strangely lit, the Rover sending out swivelling blue rays. Now Crump was ashamed of himself for enjoying the scene.

"Worn yourself quite a little path," the detective said. "Prints everywhere. Too many prints. Walk to one side, don't walk on any tracks. That's the way, keep well to one side, trespassers will be prosecuted."

"We cross the hedge here," Crump said. "Sort of scramble through. I'll show you."

"*Don't!*" said the detective. "Get back! More torches! Well, just look at that!"

The discs of light slid from one mark to another; from a long, skidding scuff in the earth to a mash of prints.

The detective said, "Do you lot lark about

49

here? Push each other to see who's going to be first across, that sort of thing? You don't? Of course you don't. I never thought you did. You proceed in an orderly manner. You're mature citizens."

He was talking to himself, Crump could tell. His mind was on the prints. "Any of you wear boots, shoes or other footwear that size?" said the detective, spotlighting big foot-prints. "Don't answer me. Of course you don't. And see how that big print is on top of a smaller one."

"Merriboots," Butterfly said. "The smaller print is Merriboots. I've got a pair just like that."

"Cordon off this area!" the detective shouted over his shoulder to the driver. "Photographer tomorrow first light, under-stood? Right. And we'll cross this hedge somewhere else. Show us where, Crump."

They walked up the final shallow rise lead-ing to the barn. "Keep to one side," the detec-tive told them. "Do not follow your natural inclinations. Do not take the shortest path between two points. And shine your torches. Ah..."

He studied the ground. "Ah, old Bigboots again. And Miss Merriboots too, digging her heels in. All clear as mud, no need to waste time on it, let's get on." He half walked, half trotted to the barn.

Crump said, "Talk about tracks! Look at this lot!"

"Proper old rally," the detective said, shining his torch from one set of tracks to another.

"Goodyear, Michelin," the driver muttered.

"Right, into the barn," said the detective. He jabbed a finger at Crump. "You stay here on the outside with Madame Butterfly. Stay here until I call you, if I call you. And keep your eyes open all the time. Never know what might pop out of an old barn."

He and the driver vanished into the barn. Outside in the dark, Butterfly and Crump could hear their footsteps and muffled words and see fans of light leak from the rotten boards that made the walls. Once, there was a frantic scuttling sound and two enormous rats hurtled out of the wall, right in front of Crump and Butterfly. They ran so hard that their feet made a little pounding noise. Like a girl in the comics, Butterfly went, "Eeek!" then laughed, shamefacedly.

"Don't blame you," Crump sympathized. He liked her.

From inside the barn came thumps and dragging sounds as the detective and the driver kicked and pulled things aside. Then, "Oy-oy!" said the driver, very loudly. "Take a look!" Crump put his cheek against the dew-wet wall to hear more. There was the sound of wood creaking. The detective said, "Get something-or-other to use as a lever... No, wait, this'll do..." Crump imagined him picking up one of the blacksmith's old bits and pieces that littered the barn.

Nails squawked in wood; wood splintered.

"Well, well, well!" said the detective's voice. "Goodness gracious me! I am surprised! Are you surprised, driver? Don't answer: you *are* surprised. You hadn't expected this, don't tell me you had. You are *surprised*. Isn't police work interesting?"

Butterfly tried to hold him back, but Crump ran into the barn. "What is it?" he said.

"A surprise," said the detective, blocking with his body Crump's view of whatever it was. "And out you go, double-quick!"

"Do what Detective Inspector Pollitt tells you," said Butterfly, primly.

So Crump saw nothing. The only thing he learned was the detective's name and rank: Mr Pollitt, Detective Inspector.

Horrie's Fag End

Horrie could not sleep. He lay in bed despising himself for being useless and idle. Crump had done something, accomplished something: he had found Shanta's flutes. But Horrie had just hung about – hung about some more – and gone to bed.

Outside, an early bird stood on a branch bellowing unmusically. Horrie reflected that the bird probably weighed about half an ounce, yet could fly, walk, feed, breed and make enough noise to deafen you. You had to admire it. You could not admire Horrie.

The first light of dawn entered his room like a thief. It stole through his eyelids and made sly suggestions: Look at me! it hinted. I'm sketching the outlines of your Empire typewriter! Why haven't you finished mending me? Or, Look at me! I'm a bottle of watchmaker's oil! Why haven't you corked me properly?

The strongest hint of all was, Isn't it time you got up and *did* something to help Shanta? Horrie rose from his bed, dressed, made faces at himself in the cracked mirror over his workbench and left the house.

Now it was really dawn, brilliant and golden. The brightness only made Horrie more miserable. He walked towards the barn,

WCHQ, scowling. He reached it and stared at it. Go on, then! he told himself. You're a clever little fellow! You're a little wonder, you are! Do something wonderful! Make a search! Go over the barn with a fine tooth comb! All the best detectives use fine tooth combs!

Searching the interior took about forty minutes. He covered every inch. His one discovery, after all this fine-tooth combing, was a coarse-toothed comb with grey muck between the teeth. He recognized it as a long-lost possession of his own.

He went outside into the sunlight, which was sharp, slanting and 3-D. Each blade of grass seemed brilliant and distinct. If there was anything to find, now was the time to find it.

He found a cigarette end.

"Oh, big deal!" he said to himself. "Terrific! You've found a fag end! Never mind about Sherlock Holmes, what about Sherlock Horrie?"

Despite his self-disgust, he picked up the fag end and studied it. He remembered that Sherlock Holmes could identify the ash of a hundred-and-something different tobaccos. Sherlock Horrie should be able to deduce something from this fag end.

All he learned was that cigarette ends left lying about in the damp turn yellowy-ginger.

It was not much of a discovery and it

seemed even smaller when two policemen appeared from nowhere and loomed over him, grinning. One of them said, "And what are you up to, young sir?"

"Nothing. Just looking around, hoping to find..."

"Ah yes. Quite understand. But frankly, Maurice —"

"My name is Horrie."

"Of course. Horrie. Well, Horrie, it might be best if you left it all to us. The professionals, you know. So if you don't mind..."

Horrie went away, walking stiffly because he could feel the policemen's eyes boring into his back.

The fag end, forgotten, lay in the gritty fluff of his jacket pocket.

The Purring Car

Shanta kept walking. Cars kept not turning up to give her a lift.

This was annoying, because quite often she heard cars – even saw their headlamps a long way away. "Must be turning off somewhere," she said aloud. "A bigger road, further back. And here's me going the wrong way."

She stopped walking and stared into the darkness, in the direction of the car noises. She did not mind the dark – indeed, she found it more friendly than the sound of her own footsteps on the tarmac. She was used to the complete dark of the countryside. Even as a very little girl, she knew all about ice-rimed grass in cold blue moonlight – about creak-ing, dripping trees in night-time forests – about bats squeaking like little ghosts and invisible cows that suddenly became huge and visible right in front of you, staring at you like outraged schoolteachers.

There had always been four of them. The four had been allowed to know these things because there were four of them. "All right, you can go out," the parents said, "as long as you stick together, understand? You *stick together*."

It was the easiest thing in the world to obey the words; because the four of them seemed

56

stuck together by some higher power almost from birth. It was only quite recently that any one of the four had even thought about this. Shanta thought about it now. I've never been alone before, she thought. Not really alone, like this. But then, I'm not really alone, I can sort of feel them *thinking* of me...

There was a car in the distance. Shanta saw its headlamps making rising and falling patterns. Perhaps this time it would not turn off. She stood in the middle of the road willing the car to come to her.

It seemed to get her message. It kept coming to her. Shanta saw the car's headlamps rise and fall, nearer and nearer, brighter and brighter. She waved.

Now the car was so close that she could hear the hum of its tyres as well as the smooth, low purr of its engine. Another bend ... just one more bend ... and it would be there! A car with a heater and soft seats and comfortable little lights glowing on the dashboard! A car to take her home!

She stood on tiptoe and waved furiously.

The car threw moving fingers of light through the hedgerow as it took the final bend and came into plain view – two brilliant white eyes that couldn't possibly miss her!

Then the brakes made the tyres chirp, the engine said, *Whoopee!* as the driver changed down smartly – and there it was, a shining saloon car whose smooth sides nudged her thigh as it halted.

The car's engine made soothing noises to itself. The driver's window gave a gentle electric whirr and slid down three inches. A man's voice said, "Want a lift? Hop in, then!"

The back door opened. Shanta hopped in at the back seat. Warmth and softness welcomed her.

So did the other occupant of the back seat.

"Hello!" he said, smiling a quick, square smile. "Just the person we've been looking for!"

Mr Brasen.

"Let me out!" Shanta croaked. Her voice was so shaky that she hardly heard her own words. "I'm getting out!"

"This is a three-litre BMW," Mr Brasen said. "Does about a hundred and thirty. At the moment, we're doing only about sixty —"

"Sixty-five," said the driver.

"Sixty-five," said Mr Brasen. "My error. You want to get out? Then get out. Go on, I dare you."

"The police know where I am," Shanta said, knowing as she spoke how stupid she sounded.

"Then they know more than I do," said Mr Brasen. "Where are we, driver?" The driver shrugged. Mr Brasen said, "There you are, you see. He doesn't know where he is. He only knows where he's going."

"You'll have to let me go *some* time," Shanta said.

"You're quite right, girlie. This year, next year, some time, never."

"But what good am I to you?" Shanta said.

"No good at all," Mr Brasen replied. "You're just a B nuisance if you'll pardon my French." Till now, his voice had been light and nasty. It became heavy and nasty. "You're a flaming nuisance!" he spat at her. "Have been all along! So go on — get out, get out! Open the door and jump!"

He sat back and was silent. The driver turned his head and said, "I reckon about ten minutes." Mr Brasen grunted. The driver said, "What are you going to do about *her*, then?"

Mr Brasen said, "None of your business." A little radio thing bleeped. Mr Brasen answered it briefly. "Yes, got her," he said. The lorry, of course! Shanta thought. That was how Mr Brasen had tracked her down. He was radio-linked to the lorry.

To Shanta, he said, "Lean right forward and put your arms behind your back. Come on, come on... No, cross your wrists. That's it. Hold still." He tied her wrists with the thin scarf he wore. It felt like silk.

The driver said, "We're there. What do you want me to do, drive right up to her?"

"Do what I told you. Drive to the sock, back up against it, turn off your lights. When Dave tells you, give us full headlights for the whole run. Then get the hell out, ditch the car and take the train to Liverpool or whatever crummy place you've chosen. You take the train, understand? Not this car. You ditch the car. And keep your mouth shut."

"Well, thank *you*," the driver said. "It's been a pleasure dealing with you, I'm sure." Sulkily, expertly, he drove the car over a field. Shanta could see long grass, then shorter grass. The car stopped. Mr Brasen got out and walked away, then stood staring into the distance. The driver muttered to Shanta, "Look, miss, don't get clever with Mr Brasen, all right? He's quite nasty, you know."

Mr Brasen came back and spoke to the driver through the window. "Don't forget, now, use the headlamps for as long as it takes, then get out and ditch the car. And keep your mouth shut, or I'll have your skin."

"I'll have my money," the driver said.

Mr Brasen gave the driver an envelope. The driver opened it and riffled through the notes inside. "What, no luncheon vouchers?" he said.

Mr Brasen told Shanta, "Get out." He hustled her through the damp grass. They passed a windsock. It was almost slack.

There was an aeroplane, a neat twin-

60

engined plane, looking big in the darkness. Inside, it was cramped and noisy – the engines had suddenly come to life. There were four men, their faces strangely lit by a single small bulb in the ceiling, grouped round a mound of packages in the centre. Shanta instantly recognized the packages. Medicines. Same as in the lorry.

"Money," the pilot said. He was a small, shabby, heavily moustached man of middle age. He took a fat envelope from Mr Brasen's hands.

Mr Brasen said, "I've dealt with some sharks in my time, but you're just about the greediest."

The pilot, unmoved, replied, "Watch your tongue, Mr Brasen. Talk like that could be bad medicine for you." He emphasized the words "bad medicine".

One of Mr Brasen's men sniggered; Mr Brasen snarled at him and the man shut up.

Shanta made a mental note.

"Come on!" Mr Brasen said to the pilot. "Let's get weaving!"

The pilot unhurriedly went on counting his money. "First things first," he said. Shanta caught the cold enmity of his voice.

"So you don't mind taking my money?" Mr Brasen sneered.

"Filthy lucre for a dirty business," the pilot said. Shanta made another mental note. The notes were adding up to a definite theme.

"Let's get on!" Brasen said, loudly.

The pilot finished counting his money, stuffed it into his jacket and said, "It's usual to strap yourself in. At least strap the *girl* in, I don't want her coming to harm. But as for you, Mr Brasen —"

"Watch your tongue if you want to do business with me again!" said Mr Brasen.

"You must be joking," the pilot said, coldly. He revved the motor and checked illuminated dials. Mr Brasen jerked straps over Shanta and tightened them. He was in a fury.

Then the plane's engines roared at full strength and the field outside and the interior of the aircraft were flooded with light from the BMW's headlamps – and they were moving over bumpy ground, thumping and shuddering – and then there were fewer bumps – no bumps at all – and Shanta's stomach felt strange...

"Off we go into the wild blue yonder," the pilot said in his cold, scornful voice. "On another of your missions of mercy, Mr Brasen."

Mr Brasen growled something, then said, in Shanta's ear. "Pill. So that you won't get air sick." He thrust a capsule at her mouth.

"I don't want a pill —"

"Yes, you do. Open your mouth."

"I don't *need* a pill —"

Mr Brasen's left hand seized Shanta's jaw. It became a vice that forced her mouth open. His right hand thrust in the pill.

"Swallow. Go on, swallow." His finger and thumb were on her throat. Please, no! Shanta thought; it's sure to be a poison pill, a killer pill, a Brasen special ...

"Go on. I want to feel you swallow. Swallow!"

She swallowed. "Where are you taking me?" she said. "Where? Why?"

"Go to sleep," he said.

"I don't want to sleep."

But surprisingly soon she wanted, more than anything in the world, to sleep... sleep... sleep...

She fell sideways, snoring. Mr Brasen saw and lifted an eyebrow. "Spark out," he said.

Incident Room

"Incident Room..." Mrs Patel said, hopelessly. "I am sorry ... what is this Incident Room? I want my daughter back, I do not know about any room..."

"Incident Room," said Mr Pollitt, speaking with his head very close to Mrs Patel's and one of her hands held in both of his. "Instant Response Unit. We're setting things up to get your daughter back, Mrs Patel. Can we use a room here? We need some space, you see, to set up our gear."

"Space," said Mrs Patel, shaking her head, barely hearing. Mr Patel, his face haunted, said, "You do what is best, Mr Pollitt. Anything. Space, anything." He too was completely lost.

Mr Bonnard, whom Crump had seen walking with his wife in the direction of the little store, came to the rescue. "Set up your Incident Room in my house," he told Mr Pollitt. "It's only just down the road. Follow me. What do you need?"

Mr Pollitt told him as they walked down the dark road. "What we do," he said, "is follow procedures. Local police call in CID and Duty Officer – that's me and my team. Right. See that Transit van following us? Full of communications gear. We can call on anything we want. Communications Centre. Control Centre. (Ah, there's the dogs! In that van. Dogs, handlers. Very useful.) We can work entirely from the van: but if you'll give us the use of part of your house – cup of tea, usual facilities, more space…"

"Anything you want," said Mr Bonnard. "The house is yours."

"Those poor Patels…" said Mrs Bonnard, shakily.

The Transit van swung into the little driveway in front of the Bonnards' house. As soon as the van stopped, it came alive: inside it, lights shone, people moved, voices mumbled, telephones trilled, electronic devices squeaked, a portable generator chuntered.

Out of the darkness, two policemen wearing gumboots half ran, half walked into the light. The men were towed along by two Alsatian dogs. The dogs' eyes shone with an almost greedy intelligence. "They know something's up," Mr Pollitt said. "The dogs always know."

A Panda car scrunched into the drive. A head poked out of its front window and said things to Mr Pollitt. "Not till dawn," Mr Pollitt told the head. "Crack of dawn, yes, certainly. Usual procedures, right?"

"Right," said the head. And the Panda was gone.

"Helicopter search," Mr Pollitt explained

to the Bonnards. "Very useful thing, your helicopter." It was cold. He drew the collar of his thornproof coat closer about his neck and smacked his lips. Mrs Bonnard took the hint. Soon, everyone had hands clasped round mugs of tea.

"Shanta, poor Shanta," Mrs Bonnard said. "Oh, Mr Pollitt, she will be found, won't she?"

But Mr Pollitt said, "Excuse me. Chief Superintendent!" And disappeared in the direction of a big Rover: so Mrs Bonnard's question was answered by Policeman 332S, who had magically taken Mr Pollitt's place. "If she can be found, ma'am, Mr Pollitt will find her," 332S told Mrs Bonnard. "Very sharp, Mr Pollitt is."

Mrs Bonnard peered up into his face, wanting to believe him. She bred King Charles spaniels and her eyes were round and brown and shining, like her dogs'.

"Very sharp *indeed*," said 332S flatly. "Believe me."

For a moment, Mrs Bonnard felt relieved: almost cheerful. But then Shanta suddenly appeared in her mind — Shanta running, with her black hair streaming, at the head of a bouncing, tumbling line of ecstatic King Charles spaniels (for Shanta helped out in the kennels in school holidays); Shanta crying, when three of a litter of puppies died; Shanta

up a tree in the orchard, throwing down
Bramley cookers for her husband to catch,
laughing when he dropped one.

So *alive* ... thought Mrs Bonnard. But
now... And Mrs Bonnard's round, brown
eyes clouded with tears.

Home Sweet Home

"Look alive!" said Mr Brasen. He shook Shanta's shoulder. She was deep in her drugged sleep. "We're there!" said Mr Brasen. "Get up and get out."

It was daylight. The sun was low yet the air was already oven-hot. She stumbled out of the little aircraft, getting jostled by the men who were unloading the plane's cargo of packages. When they finished their work, they sat in the plane.

Shanta stood on hard, rocky ground, still warm from yesterday's sun. Ahead of her stretched an old, empty runway. The concrete was broken. Skimpy flowers and weeds pushed up through the cracks. Beyond, she saw twisted trees with small, dark green leaves; and more rocks, and very little else.

If there was little to see, there was plenty to smell. Shanta's nose twitched. It was a hot, foreign, spicy smell, bittersweet, with a hint of flowers.

What flowers? She tried to name them – but her head ached, her mind worked only slowly. And then the aircraft roared and turned through one hundred and eighty degrees, its propeller flung grit in her face and eyes. It roared louder still, then rushed along the runway, faster and faster. Shanta wanted to read the numbers on its fuselage, but the plane was going straight into the sun, she could see nothing but glare through her gritty eyes.

Now the aircraft was free of the runway. It did not turn and circle, it just headed straight into the sun, growing smaller and smaller until it was a pretty toy, a perfect model aeroplane.

She had learned nothing about it. She could not give it a name. Her brain was lead and her eyes felt muddy.

"That way," said Mr Brasen, pushing her ahead of him with his hard hand. She started walking, feeling the sun's heat grow stronger with every step.

"Where am I?" she said.

"Where you belong," said Mr Brasen.

"I belong at home, in England! I don't feel well —"

"Keep walking. And shut up."

She obeyed, but minutes later she once again demanded, "Where am I?"

"I told you. Where you belong. You're in India."

"I don't belong in India! I'm British, I was born in England!"

"Well, now you're in India. You'd better learn to like it. See that? Over there? That's your new home."

He stopped walking, jerked Shanta to a halt by tugging her hair, and whistled sharply

69

through his teeth. Ahead of them lay a pile of rocks with a black hole in it. The pile of rocks was, Shanta saw, a sort of cottage with a doorway. You would never have taken it for a human dwelling-place but for some washing dangling from a line. Children's clothing.

"Home sweet home," said Mr Brasen. He whistled again and grumbled, "Come *on*, come *on*."

A woman came out of the black hole that was the doorway. Her skin was so dark that it was almost black. She lifted her head and yelled something in reply to Mr Brasen's whistle. The sound she made was like an animal's.

"Make yourself at home," said Mr Brasen, giving Shanta a violent shove towards the woman. Then he turned his back on her and walked off.

The woman made a clawing gesture that meant, Come here. Shanta obeyed. Her head ached so badly that her eyes were affected: the rocks often seemed to grow fringes of colour round them and the blue sky kept turning a blinding white. But now she was being pulled through the black hole, into the darkness inside the cottage.

The woman was screeching at her but Shanta did not understand the ugly sounds she made. Yet she saw, as if through a magnifying glass, that the woman's mouth had only five front teeth, two in the upper jaw and three in the lower. *Five* teeth. Exactly *five*. You must remember that, she told herself.

Her legs gave way: she fell on her knees, her head spinning and felt the woman's bare foot push against her ribs. She let herself fall sideways and landed on top of two bodies. Children. The children squeaked and squawked at her. They pushed at her with warm, sticky hands. It was too dark for Shanta to see them and in any case her eyes were not working properly.

"Drugged, he drugged me," she said.

Then, "*Five* teeth, *two* children."

Then nothing.

Cur Faytew Dank!

When she awoke, it was afternoon. The scorching sun was almost overhead. The children were outside, playing. Their hoarse, harsh voices wakened Shanta. Or perhaps it was the bellowing screech of their mother – the woman with five front teeth; the children were at some distance; the woman stood outside the doorway, yelling at them.

The words she used were soon to become familiar to Shanta. Now she heard them for the first time...

"CUR FAYTEW DANK! EH! CUR FAYTEW DANK!"

The woman had a voice like a band-saw and the stink in the hovel was awful. So Shanta scrambled on hands and knees through the low doorway and stood in the glare outside, blinking. At once, the heat of the sun hit her. She felt prickles of sweat jump from her skin. She had never guessed that the sun could be so hot.

But this was India.

She looked at India and India glared back at her, raw and rocky and rough. India wasn't as she had expected it to be from pictures in magazines. Those pictures showed India as dusty and golden, crowded with thin-legged men in dhotis and women in saris with little bangles round their wrists.

Oh, come on! Shanta told herself, What do you know about India? It's a whole *continent*, not just a little country. Yet, all the same, this place surprised her.

The woman and children surprised her too. The woman did not wear a sari: she was dressed in a miserable looking print frock. On her head she wore nothing. Around her ankles coiled rolled-down stockings. On her feet she wore plastic sandals of a sickly yellow colour. There was nothing Indian-looking about her except her dark skin.

The children were almost naked. There were three of them, not two: a beautiful little girl with black, greasy ringlets, wide, wild, animal eyes and a runny nose. The two boys were – what was the best word? – *hard*. Little bunchy muscles jumped under their dirty brown skins – skins that wouldn't cut or bruise easily. Their voices were like the cawing of crows. And indeed the bigger of the two boys was tearing a dead bird to pieces – it could have been a crow – throwing tattered clumps of feathers at the smaller boy, who tried to snatch the corpse for himself. It was a brutal game, brutally played.

"*Cur faytew dank!*" the mother screeched at them. They took no notice. Now the big boy had found out how to squeeze the skull of the bird so that the beak gaped. He

73

advanced on the small boy, trying to frighten him. It did not work. The smaller boy just tried to grab the skull.

"Five ... eight ... ten," Shanta said to herself, guessing the three children's ages. The woman made hard, grunting noises and seized Shanta's left boot. She pulled it off. Then the right. Now Shanta was barefoot. The ground hurt her feet.

"Aii-ee! Monje!" yelled the woman, beating an iron pot with an iron ladle. The children rushed into the hovel and came out with tin plates in their hands. The woman threw some sort of stew into their plates. Without looking at Shanta, she got a plate for her and thrust it, heaped with dark, greasy stuff, into her hands. Then she handed out lumps of bread torn off a long loaf.

The children used the bread to scoop the food into their mouths. Shanta imitated them. She was not very surprised at this way of eating. She knew that in India, it was quite usual to use chapattis – flat discs of un-leavened bread – to hold mouthfuls of food. Properly done, it was a tidy, sensible way to eat. But these Indians bolted their food: their cheeks and noses became smeared with grease.

The food tasted as bad as it looked. There wasn't even any rice – Indian food without rice! – nor a hint of curry. But Shanta ate everything she was given. She felt weak and guessed that she would need strength.

Nobody spoke much during the meal. There was lots of noise but none of it was speech. Sometimes the mother screeched, *"Cur faytew dank!"* when one child tried to steal another's bread; sometimes the boys would fly at each other, squawking, for no obvious reason. The little girl just ate and ate, then silently held out her plate for more.

When everyone was stuffed and sweating, each person went his or her way. Nobody spoke to or even looked at Shanta, until the little girl began staring. She simply stared, as a cat stares, with emotionless, impersonal eyes. Shanta soon got used to it.

Shanta told herself, Now is the time to escape. I'll just get up and go. I'll keep walking until I meet some proper Indian people — people who have nothing to do with Mr Brasen.

She got up and started walking.

Now, everyone noticed her! The woman screeched, *"AI! EH! CUR FAYTEW DANK!"* The boys turned to stare at her, their eyes the only clean things in their dusty, sweaty faces. Then they bent down and began picking up rocks.

Shanta kept walking. She stared straight ahead.

The first rock bounced harmlessly along the ground, quite close to her. She kept walking.

The second rock, a small piece, hit her lightly between the shoulder blades. She kept walking.

The third rock laid open the flesh of her left leg. Blood spurted and ran down over her ankle bone. The sun was so hot that it dried almost immediately. Shanta limped on.

Suddenly the bigger boy appeared right in front of Shanta. He must have run silently in half a circle to cut her off. Shanta halted. The boy stretched out his hard, thin arm and showed her the rock in his hand. The rock was big and jagged. Shanta felt her head spin with fear.

The boy came closer. He jerked the rock as if to push it into her face – and at the same time, lifted his right leg and kicked Shanta in the stomach. His bare foot felt as hard as a fist. She fell down, gasping with pain and shock.

The boy pointed to the hovel. Shanta went to it. The woman, her hands on her hips, silently pointed to the doorway. Shanta bent down and entered the darkness.

Soon the girl child appeared in the doorway and stayed there, staring expressionlessly and occasionally wiping her nose with the back of her pretty little hand. She watched without much interest as Shanta wept. She wept not with pain, but with hopelessness. She would never escape from India, she knew that now.

She knew it all the better when night came and it was time to sleep. The woman had found a length of thin cable – it looked like part of the wiring of a car. She tied one end of the cable round Shanta's ankle and the other round the bigger boy's. This done, she made a satisfied clucking sound and smacked Shanta's face by way of goodnight.

Everyone slept. Everyone but Shanta.

The Vigil

Jen said, "It's stupid, I can't stand any more of it!" The three WCs were sitting on a low wall facing the Bonnards' house. "Hanging around all day, not *doing* anything. Sorry, but I'm off. Goodbye."

Crump caught her arm. "Look, you never know, they might get some news. Something might happen. I mean, we've *got* to stick around, it's only decent!"

"Decent! Oh, gollygosh, must do the decent thing, demmit!" said Jen. She jerked her arm free and walked off, her back straight and her long blonde hair swinging indignantly.

Horrie said, "Well, that's girls for you. No time for Shanta: too busy thinking about her posh holiday in the South of *Frar-arnce*. Makes you sick."

Crump said, "Oh, I don't know. I mean, what good are we doing just being here? We're only getting in the way of *them*." He nodded his head at the Incident Room.

The three remaining WCs had haunted the place ever since Shanta's disappearance. "It's a sort of vigil," Horrie had said, in a hushed voice, on the first day. But this was the third day.

Horrie said, "Bet you it rains within the hour." Then, "Wonder what Jen's up to."

"Gone with her parents to deliver that stupid gee-gee. Off in a Range Rover to a place near Folkestone. Horse in the trailer behind, with its tail hanging over the door. Holding up the traffic. Stupid *horses*! I mean, fancy using a *car* to transport a *horse*! It doesn't make sense."

Mr Pollitt, wearing his thornproof coat, swished up to the Bonnards' house in a big Ford. He saw Crump and Horrie and said, "What? Still here? It's going to rain."

"We know," Horrie said, without moving.

"Well ... be it on your head. The rain, I mean," said Mr Pollitt, and disappeared into the Incident Room van.

It began to rain. "Told you it would," Horrie said to Crump.

Crump said, "Oh, put that thing away! It's boring, bor-ing!"

He was referring to Horrie's pendulum. The pendulum was a brass bobweight, a ball about an inch in diameter, with a point sticking out of its tail end. It dangled from a long piece of string.

Horrie said, "Don't knock my pendulum. I got a twitch out of it last night. It swung in a cross, it was fantastic. I'd got it hung over the map of England, and I was concentrating like mad on old Shanta – holding that woolly hat of hers in my hand, you have to hold a personal possession – and sure enough it started swinging in a cross! Oh, I know you don't believe me —"

"I don't. I don't believe in pendulums, poltergeists, pixies, seeing the future in tea-leaves ... anything. I don't even believe in Santa Claus. So you know what you can do with your pendulum."

"It swung in a cross, back and forth! It did, honest!" Horrie said.

"OK, it swung in a cross! Perhaps you were looking at it cross-eyed! Ho, ho, jolly joke. *Where* did it swing in a cross?"

"In my bedroom. It was late, I was —"

"I don't mean what *room*, stupid. I mean what part of the map. Where does your piffling pendulum say Shanta is?"

"Oh. In the south-east. It did its cross over Kent. Look, there are lots of well authenticated cases of lost and murdered people being found by mediums using pendulums. I can show you the books. I've been reading up on it —"

"You and your books. *Exactly* where in Kent? I mean, just saying 'south-east' doesn't help much."

"Well, it was quite near Folkestone."

"Folkestone! Folkestone, was it? My, my, what a coincidence! How astonishing!"

"What do you mean?"

"Well, Folkestone's the last place we mentioned, isn't it? The place where Jen's heading

80

for. I wonder what put the word Folkestone into your furry little head, Horrie?"

"The pendulum put it into my head! Anyhow, it wasn't Folkestone itself, it was a place just near it, as far as I could see —"

"As far as you could see. Ho, hum."

"No, seriously. You can't tell exactly, everything's swinging about, but it looked like a place called Hookham, a small place."

"Horrie, you're a nutter."

"All right, I'm a nutter. But the pendulum told me Hookham – at least, I think it did."

"I wonder what the pendulum would say," Crump said, "if *I* held it? I mean, it might take off and go into orbit if *I* held it. You see, I've got these amazing powers – super-duper spooky powers!" He grabbed at the pendulum.

"Leave go of it, you'll break the string. Look, if you really want to try it, try it! I'm not stopping you. Come home with me: give it a go. What have you got to lose?"

"All right, I will. Lead on, you poor old nutter."

They walked through the rain to Horrie's home.

The Vision

The horse had its tail hanging out of the trailer, just as Crump had said. There were still many miles between the horse and Folkestone.

Jen said to her father, "I shouldn't have come, I should have stayed with Horrie and Crump."

Her father didn't condescend to answer. Her mother – Jen was crushed between the two of them in the Range Rover – said, "We didn't exactly *beg* you to come, sweetie. But you're here, aren't you? So please don't start *moaning*. Have a peppermint and don't *moan*."

"I don't want a peppermint. And I'm not moaning. But I do feel a bit ill."

Her father said, "Don't be ill on me. Where are we, Fi?" Fiona, his wife, looked at the map and said, "Haven't a clue. Oh, wait... I think the next village will be Bookham."

"Don't be silly, Bookham's in Surrey. We're in Kent."

"Yes, of course. Such tiny print. We go through Hookham, turn left and left again, and then it's about ten miles. Jen, you're not really going to be ill, are you? I'm rather *hoping* to make a good impression on these people."

"I'm not that sort of ill," Jen said. "Just not well."

"Well, I wish you wouldn't look so *white*."

"I feel rather white. Just leave me alone, Mummy."

Jen was left alone with her thoughts. They puzzled her. Not *white,* she thought, I'm feeling *dark*. And not glowing dark, like Shanta, but dark like a dark night. The dead of night. And I'm alone...

She made herself concentrate on the blurred views flashing by. Fences, trees, houses, telephone wires, birds flying...

Birds flying? No, something bigger than a bird. And in the dark, not in the daytime. She, Jen, was in this flying thing, rushing through darkness! No, that was wrong, it wasn't her, it was someone else...

Shanta.

"Jen, sit up *straight* and have a *peppermint!*" said her mother's voice, very loudly.

"Ah, Hookham!" said her father. "There's the sign. Good. We'll be there on the dot."

They arrived at the stroke of noon and delivered the horse to its new owners. Their daughter was called Sally. She and Jen got along like a house on fire. Jen forgot about darkness and flying and being Shanta.

But later, she remembered.

Codswallop

Even later that evening, in WCHQ, Horrie and Crump still argued about the pendulum. When Jen – just back from Kent – came into the barn to ask the latest news of the search for Shanta, the two boys were hunched over their map. The pendulum hung over the map from a tripod of sticks.

"What's going on?" Jen demanded.

"Oh, nothing," Horrie said. "It's just that poor little Crumpie-wumpie can't trust his wee peepers any more." Horrie patted Crump's hair. Crump lashed out backhanded at Horrie, but missed.

"You see, Jen," Horrie continued, "this morning we played pendulums, and it was *ever* so nice because Crump made the pendulum do exactly the things I told him it would do. Twice. The same things I'd done. But Crump didn't want to believe his own eyes – did you, Crumpie? – and he got in *such* a naughty temper..."

Again Crump tried to hit Horrie. Again he missed. He said to Jen, "It's all a load of codswallop, Jen." His voice was gloomy and defensive as he explained.

Jen listened intently, then said, "So you hung the pendulum on this tripod so that it couldn't cheat – I mean, your hands couldn't influence it?"

"That's right," Crump admitted.

"And it still worked? It still pointed at a place called Hookham?"

"No, that's what Horrie says! But I say it was just a sort of trick of the light or something like that! And it only did it twice, it won't do it now —"

"Never mind that," Jen said. "The place it pointed at was Hookham? H,o,o,k,h —"

"It was Hookham. So far, the pendulum's pointed to Hookham four times."

"Of course, it's all codswallop... Don't have anything to do with it, Jen."

"I don't have to," Jen said, in a tone of voice that made both boys look up at her face. "You see, I know about Hookham. We passed through Hookham today. And something happened to me."

"What sort of thing?" Crump said.

"I don't know... Something odd. Stupid, perhaps. Here, give me that thing, I want a go. What do you do?"

"Just put your hands on the top of the tripod and concentrate. Here, hold on to Shanta's hat."

"Concentrate on what?" Jen asked.

"On Shanta, of course, what else? Go on, get on with it."

She put her hands on the tripod. Crump kicked the pendulum lightly to make it swing.

He said, "It works better if you close your eyes. *Really* concentrate." His voice was gruff and embarrassed.

The pendulum swung more or less in a circle. Jen closed her eyes.

The pendulum swung in a narrow oblong. Jen thought of Shanta and clutched the hat.

The pendulum swung in a straight line. Jen whispered, "Anything happening?"

Impossibly, the pendulum swung in a cross. "Keep at it!" Horrie told Jen, hoarsely.

"You can open your eyes now, and look," Crump said, half a minute later. The pendulum was still swinging, quite strongly. Swinging in a cross, over a certain place on the map.

Jen looked, with her nose almost touching the map. "*Hookham!*" she whispered.

She told Crump and Horrie about her flying-through-darkness vision in the Range Rover. Horrie said, "It could still be codswallop... Yes, I know the pendulum thing was my idea, but now I don't trust it." He was suddenly deeply dejected and pessimistic.

"A moment ago, you were sending me up for not believing in the pendulum!" Crump said.

"I know. But when you think about it... it's not scientific, it's got to be codswallop."

Jen picked at her lower lip, coming to a decision. "We're going to see Mr Pollitt!" she announced.

"What for?" said Horrie.

"To deliver some codswallop," said Jen.

Mr Pollitt was gone and wouldn't return till morning. "Come back then," said the policemen in the Incident Room.

"Better hurry home," they added, looking at the sky.

Sure enough, the drizzle became steady rain. The WCs hunched their shoulders and made their various ways home. Horrie went slower than the others: he wanted to get wet, wanted to become even more depressed. Pendulums and Funny Feelings! Kids' stuff! Fine help they were being! And all the time poor Shanta...

He stuffed his hands deep in his pockets, and his fingertips touched the fag end.

He'd forgotten it. Which was not surprising. It was hardly worth remembering. All the same, it was something you could see and touch, something Mr Pollitt should see and touch.

He'd get to Mr Pollitt first thing in the morning, before Jen and Crump had a chance to go raving on about Pendulums and Funny Feelings.

*   *   *

87

He was lucky. Just before eight next morning, he caught Mr Pollitt standing outside the Incident Room. Mr Pollitt was smoking a small cigar. He was too polite to smoke in the Bonnards' house.

"Ah, young Horrie," said Mr Pollitt. "Caught me having a crafty drag. Stupid habit. A fool at one end, a fire at the other. Anything on your mind?"

"I found something," Horrie mumbled. "Might be a clue. I mean, you never know. In detective stories, even the smallest things turn out to be important."

"Ah, detective stories," said Mr Pollitt. "Oh yes, oh yes indeed. The bumbling police get it all wrong and the amateur sleuth solves the mystery." He sighed, then said, "I heard you were doing a bit of detective work the other day, right? Crack of dawn, up at the barn?"

Horrie nodded miserably.

"Well, it's a free country," said Mr Pollitt. "Did you make any startling discoveries?"

"All I got," Horrie said, "was wet feet and – this."

"A cigarette end," said Mr Pollitt. "Dear me, we should have spotted that. Well, well, well."

He pulled out the tweezers from a little army knife and began plucking at strands of tobacco. Then he said, "Well, well, well," once again. To Horrie's surprise, Mr Pollitt appeared really interested in the fag end.

"Who smoked this?" he said, in a hard tone of voice that was a second surprise for Horrie.

"I don't know," Horrie said. "I haven't a clue."

"Is that so?" Mr Pollitt said, cocking his bony head to one side and staring hard at Horrie. "You haven't a clue? Is that what you said?"

But then Jen and Crump turned up, and the sergeant called Mr Pollitt to the telephone, and there was no more talk about fag ends and smoking.

For the time being.

Swinging Scene

Mr Pollitt barred the door to the Incident Room with his body. "Bit busy," he explained. "No interruptions. Right. What *is* it?"

The WCs told him about the pendulum. The corners of Mr Pollitt's mouth twitched as he listened.

Mr Pollitt said, "No. I'm not laughing at you. Having a bit of a giggle, perhaps, but not what you'd call actually *laughing*. Go on about this pendulum of yours. Sounds a real swinging scene."

All three WCs gave Mr Pollitt the fish eye. He said, "All right, *not* funny. Now, about this pendulum?"

The WCs explained at length.

"Ah," said Mr Pollitt, too politely. "Well, fancy that. Goodness gracious."

"No, honestly. Again and again. A crisscross over a place in east Kent."

Suddenly Mr Pollitt was sitting bolt upright, eyes wide, almost comically attentive.

"Any particular *part* of east Kent?" he said. "Any place you'd care to give a *name* to?"

"Look, if you're sending us up —" Crump began.

"Oh, no! Very definitely not! I'm asking you – can you give this place a *name*?"

"Hookham," Jen said.

"*Hookham*," said Mr Pollitt. "You said *Hookham*. In east Kent. Yes?"

"Hookham," Jen repeated.

"Come inside for a moment," said Mr Pollitt. "We've got to have a little chat."

They entered the Incident Room.

The room was filled with communications gear, maps, tea mugs and tunic-less policemen. A sergeant said, "Oh, Mr Pollitt, Sir, we've just got this in from —"

"Never mind," said Mr Pollitt. "Later. Here, tape what our young friends have to tell us. Don't miss a syllable. Right, you three, start again from the beginning."

At the end, Mr Pollitt turned to the sergeant and said, "Hookham. Well, what do you make of that, Sergeant?"

"Could be a coincidence, Sir."

"And I could be a fairy queen. *Am* I a fairy queen, Sergeant?"

"Not to my knowledge, Sir."

"Well, what do we know about Hookham, Sergeant? To what conclusion have our official inquiries led us?"

"All here on the map, Sir. Derelict, unused wartime airstrip by the village. Three reports from locals, all followed up, of activity on the airfield on the night of —"

"Quite so, Sergeant. An aeroplane took off in the middle of the night from Hookham. An unidentified flying object, Sergeant. No flights OK'd by local flying clubs or anything of that sort. Just a plane taking off, a few residents disturbed by the noise, a few complaints and queries to the local cop shop. And now our young friends here have come to the same conclusion."

"It was Shanta in that plane," Jen said. "I felt it, I really did. Felt *her*. When we drove through Hookham, with the horse – I've just been telling you about it —"

"So you have," said Mr Pollitt.

"Do you *believe* us?" said Jen.

"Do we believe them, Sergeant?" said Mr Pollitt.

"Yes, Sir. We believe them."

"Why, Sergeant?"

"Well, look," the sergeant began. It took him a long time to tell the whole story of the police inquiries: the false leads, the door-to-door questionings, the police dogs following trails that led to nowhere and nothing; what CID said, what Division said; and at last, lines of inquiry that criss-crossed over a certain time, a certain place.

"It all comes down to Hookham, doesn't it?" Horrie said when the sergeant had finished. "They kidnapped Shanta and got her to Hookham and then flew her to – *where* did they fly her?"

"We've got a few ideas about that, too,"

the sergeant said. "It was a light plane, right? Light aircraft don't have a very long range. Of course, you can stop and refuel, but even then, our investigations lead us to believe that it was possibly —"

"Mr Brasen!" Jen said. "It's to do with him, and us being Worm Charmers, and him wanting us out of our HQ, his mouldy barn, and trying to get us out of the way that Friday... Oh dear, I want Shanta back!" And suddenly she was near to tears. She was better almost at once. "Mr Brasen did it," she said. "I know it. It's him."

"You're most likely right about Mr Brasen, as well as Hookham," Mr Pollitt said. "We've been looking into his business activities."

"What sort of business is he in?" Horrie said.

"Funny business," Mr Pollitt said, his face like iron. "Most amusing. You'll die laughing."

Funny Business

"What sort of funny business?" Horrie asked Mr Pollitt.

"Drugs. No, not your grass and snow and glue-sniffing kind of drugs – not the sort of drugs that turn well people into sick people. He's on to an even nastier racket than that. He turns sick people into dying people. And dying people into dead people."

"How?" said Jen.

"Sells them dud medicines. Medical drugs that kill them instead of making them better."

"I don't get it," Crump said. "I mean, you get medicines through the doctor, he writes your prescription; then the chemist sells you the medicine. So how —"

"Show 'em, Sergeant," said Mr Pollitt.

The sergeant threw down two cartons in front of the WCs. The cartons looked the same. Both were businesslike packets with a trade name, *Digitalinex,* printed big at the top and lots of small print below.

"You're seventy-seven years old," Mr Pollitt said, pointing a bony finger at Jen. "You're a nice old thing, still got lots to live for – the grandchildren coming over on Sunday and all that – but you've got heart trouble. A dicky ticker. 'Oh, Doctor, Doctor,' you say, 'I get these chest pains like a knife going through me, it frightens me to death!' 'Ah,' says the doctor. 'We can't have that, can we? Here you are, you nice old lady: *Digitalinex*!'" He tapped the cartons. "'Just keep taking the tablets and you'll be fine.' So she takes the tablets – and dies. Dies because the tablets are duds. Phonies. No-goods."

"How does Mr Brasen come into it?" Jen said.

"Ah. The doctor prescribed the right pills – *Digitalinex*. Good stuff. Works wonders. And the chemist ordered the right stuff from the right wholesalers – so-many packets of *Digitalinex*, in a carton like this." He held one of the two cartons out for Jen to see. "But something went wrong along the line, right? What would that be, do you think?"

"Mr Brasen!" Jen said.

"Forged packets," said Horrie.

"With dud pills inside them," said Crump.

"Right, right and right again," said Mr Pollitt. "Very smart of you. Very astute. Junior detectives!"

He was talking to give himself time to decide what to say next, but Jen blazed at him, "Don't treat us like … just *kids*!" she stormed. Mr Pollitt stared at her, his raised eyebrows forcing his long forehead into a dozen tight wrinkles.

"I'm not," he said. "I don't. You're not just *kids*. Not to me. And even if you were, which you're not, it wouldn't make your results less interesting. I mean, we've been making investigations the official way, and you've been doing things with pendulums and strange experiences ... but we're all running on the same lines, aren't we?"

Jen said, "I'm sorry if I was rude. It's just that... I want Shanta back so much." Suddenly she burst into noisy tears. Crump patted her back. Mr Pollitt awkwardly stroked her head and said, "There, now," several times.

Being patted and stroked both at once felt ridiculous. Jen could not help giggling through her tears. Mr Pollitt said, "All right, now?" and Jen kissed him on the cheek. The sergeant said, "Hmm!" and Mr Pollitt said, "Police Officer kissed by Glamorous Blonde. Oh yes, definitely. Any time at all."

Jen, herself again, said, "Go on about Mr Brasen and the dud drugs."

The sergeant threw some cardboard packages on the table. "Right," said Mr Pollitt. "We'll begin with these two. Identical packets of *Digitalinex,* am I right? Of course I'm right. Identical. But they're not. One's a phony, a fake. Tell me which one!"

"Can we look inside, at the pills?" Horrie asked.

"If you like, but it won't help you. All identical and all *Digitalinex. But —*"

"But what?"

"This little lot on the left is outdated stock, that's what. *Digitalinex* goes off, you see. Like eggs, or cooked meats. Starts off lovely — then becomes poisonous."

"Starts by curing, ends by killing?" Crump said.

"That's the way of it. Like roast pork. Bacon and botulism."

"And Mr Brasen..."

"Mr Brasen begs, borrows or steals outdated stuff. Even pays for it. If it's not ready-packed, he trots off to the printers for packaging, complete with recent date codes. Forged packaging for outdated pills that could kill you."

"But what's the point?" Horrie said. "I mean, how does he earn a living at it?"

"Ah! *Digitalinex* is quite a costly item. See this pill? That's 32p. See this phial of capsules? Twenty capsules, times 32p, equals 640p. But the carton contains one hundred phials, equals £640!"

"Nice money," Horrie muttered.

"Oh, nice, very nice! Makes us poor flatfoots green with envy. And he doesn't just deal in *Digitalinex*, of course. Oh dear me, no."

"Antibiotics," suggested the sergeant.

"Oh, yes indeed, antibiotics!" said Mr Pollitt. "You're a moron of twenty-three," he said, jabbing his finger at Crump. "And you've just come off your brand new super-de-luxe Yamasuki motorbike doing eighty mph where you shouldn't have been doing thirty, you silly person. So we scrape you off the tarmac and send your bits to the hospital. The kind surgeons sew all the bits together – and there you are, recovering nicely. All you need to complete your cure is a course of antibiotics. *Must* have them, otherwise you could develop all sorts of infections. Unfortunately —"

"Mr Brasen supplies dud antibiotics, so I die," said Crump.

"You do indeed."

"Developing nations," suggested the sergeant.

"Yes, you have a point there," Mr Pollitt agreed. "You see, over here, in this sceptred isle, we're very careful about what we buy. Quality control, government checks and tests, the lot.

"But poor countries can't manage things like that. And they're generally strapped for ready cash – and often in a hurry – and haven't got proper hospitals. Et cetera.

"So if *you*," Mr Pollitt said, pointing the bony finger at Horrie, "find yourself stuck in some war or earthquake or famine ... with a spear in your backside and horrible germs in your inside ... if that happens to *you*, well, it's Luck Out. They carry you, groaning something terrible, to a field hospital full of flies but empty of medical supplies. So there's an appeal, a relief fund is started. 'Do hurry, people are dying, help us send medicines'."

"And Mr Brasen happens to have medicines ready?" said Horrie.

"For instant delivery," said Mr Pollitt. "You name the medicines, he has them. His stuff will kill you, of course. It's dud. But it *looks* right. See for yourself!" He threw pairs of packets into the hands of the WCs.

"The ones we've punched a hole in are genuine," he said. "Otherwise we'd get mixed up ourselves. And even if there were differences, who's to spot them? I mean, one printer does one lot; another printer does a later batch. Different card and paper stocks, different printers' inks – bound to be differences."

"Only way is to swallow the pills," suggested the sergeant.

"Ah, that's it!" agreed Mr Pollitt. "Swallow the genuine pills, and you'll probably get better. Swallow Mr Brasen's and you'll definitely get worse. Slow death for you; quick profit for your friend Mr Brasen."

"He's not our friend!" Jen said. "I'd kill him myself if I could!"

"My mistake, my mistake," said Mr Pollitt. "Nobody's friend. The whole world's enemy. Nasty piece of work in the dirtiest trade you can think of."

He pulled at one forefinger and stared into the distance, his face as hard and sharp as a hatchet. "I wouldn't mind getting hold of Mr Brasen myself," he said.

He pulled harder at his forefinger. The joint gave a loud, unpleasant crack.

"Cup of tea," suggested the sergeant.

The Penny Drops

The sun, the sun...

Every day it seemed to burn hotter. Now the boys no longer played their brutal games in the open. They panted like dogs in the hot shade of the hot rocks, too tired even to torment each other. And for whole hours, the little girl's nose did not run; the sun had dried her up.

The woman had taken to lying in her hovel all afternoon, fanning herself with a woven fan. Shanta could see her feet. Sometimes the feet wriggled crossly. Sometimes Shanta saw the woman's hand scratching under the stockings rolled round her ankles.

If she were really asleep, I might escape, Shanta thought. If the boys slept, I could creep past them and make for that valley down there. And then...

She thought constantly of escape. It was her greatest pleasure. But now even that was taken from her because of the sun. The sun was unbearable. Shanta had the feeling that at any moment, the sky itself might burst into flames.

Then a wind came: a searing wind, hot as the blast from an oven.

A few kilometres north of Shanta, a bleached

and withered little tuft of grass smoked. A small flame shyly raised up its head – retired – popped up again for a better look – then jumped for joy. It danced, spat, spread sideways and finding nearby a twig hardly bigger than a pin, gave birth to a flame six times its own size.

This flame quivered, shivered, leaped – and exploded. A square metre of countryside was on fire.

Soon the square metre became kilometres, hectares, whole tracts of land. Now the flames were walls of fire, fields of flame, rolling columns of smoke, always advancing, always devouring.

Sirens screamed, engines howled, men came. The men shouted and flailed at the fire – smothered it with water and chemicals – beat at it, dug ditches to starve it. But the flames jumped the ditches, drank the water, laughed at the chemicals and flails.

The men gasped, sweated and stumbled back in defeat. The flames roared, spread and rolled forward to victory.

The hot wind that fed and drove forward the flames came from inland. It blew towards the sea. Between the flames and the sea lay the baking, rocky region in which Shanta was held captive.

Shanta was the last to understand what was

happening. One moment, she was pulling at her T-shirt, trying to separate it from sweat-sodden skin. Next moment, the hot wind blew and instantly dried her sweat. But there was something about the wind she did not like. It carried a strange smell; it turned the sky a weird colour. She rose to her feet, trying to stare in the direction the wind came from; but her eyes were filled with stinging grit, she had to turn away.

"*AI-EEE!*" the woman was yelling. She yelled and waved her dark, scrawny arm. "*AM-BEY-SHEEL!*" she screamed at Shanta. "*TENNAY!*" Now she was throwing things towards Shanta.

The two boys were running round like dogs, backs bent, brown paws grabbing and snatching at the things the woman threw – bits of bedding, pots and pans, anything that could be bundled and bagged and carried.

Now the mother was looking for the little girl. "*CUR FAYTEW DANK!*" she squawked, running from place to place, thrusting her nose into dark places where the child might be hiding. "*CUR FAYTEW DANK! EE-SEE, EE-SEE!*"

At that moment, the penny dropped for Shanta.

India! This wasn't India! These people weren't Indians!

The face of Mrs Loomis (French, Geography, Junior English) suddenly appeared from the past and stood before Shanta's mind's eye. *Ici*, Shanta. Say it. *Répétez ici. Ici*, Miss Loomis. It means "here".

And CUR FAYTEW DANK — that had to be *Que fais-tu donc?* The French for "What are you doing?"

And *am-bey-sheel!* was the woman's way of pronouncing *imbécile* – idiot; and *tennay!* was *tenez!* – Take hold!

Not India: France! This was France! The south of France, where the lavender came from. That accounted for the smells she had noticed from the beginning – the smell of lavender, flowers, herbs. Miss Loomis had told the class all about them. The south of France, by the Mediterranean: that was where she was!

"*Allez, allez, allez!*" the woman shouted. She had found the little girl. Now she was running and stumbling on her sturdy, bent legs, one hand clutching the child's hand, the other clawing at a huge ragged bundle on her shoulder. The smaller boy was almost hidden by his burden of possessions. He would drop something, stop running, pick it up, start running. The older boy had Shanta by the wrist. He was dragging her, wrenching her to her feet when she stumbled, swearing at her.

Shanta pulled free. She stood dazed, looking behind her, into the hot wind. The boy swore and beckoned, his bare feet shuffling with fury and impatience. She ignored him. She thought only of escape. But escape to where?

Over the rocky ridge behind her, she saw ragged little fiery devils rocket into the tiger-yellow sky. She smelled their devilish smell, understood the ferocious heat. There was no escape that way, where a raging inferno threw the fire devils into the sky. The fire devils jetted and soared, then fell like ragged birds.

Now the sky was red and its brazen heat beat at her in pulsing waves. She had to run. There was only one way to go: she had to follow her captors. She ran.

A great roll of dark smoke chased her, caught up with her, choked her, stung her with fiery particles. Shanta ran faster still.

Channels

That evening, the WCs had a long session with the pendulum. Next morning, they managed to catch Mr Pollitt.

"We think we know the place!" Jen announced.

"Hookham, you mean?" said Mr Pollitt. "That's old history."

"Not Hookham, the place where she is *now*."

"We used the pendulum on a map of Europe," Horrie explained. "Abroad. It kept swinging over the same place. Again and again. We know where she is, abroad."

"Is that so?" Mr Pollitt said. "Is that really so?"

"She's near a place called Borme," Jen said. "South of France. No, listen to us, don't pull that 'Silly Kids' face —"

"I'm not pulling faces of any kind. Definitely not."

"You mean, you believe us?"

"I'll admit, I wouldn't believe you just on the strength of that pendulum of yours. But there's also the little matter of the supporting evidence from Horrie. Important evidence. Very."

"What do you mean?" Jen said.

"This," said Mr Pollitt; and produced Horrie's cigarette end. It looked quite smart now, mounted on a piece of clean card and protected by a transparent envelope.

"Boyard," said Mr Pollitt.

"Boyard?"

"French cigarette, name of Boyard. Like your Gauloise, the ones in the blue packs. Only Boyards have an even stronger pong. And there's another thing about them: the paper. Very distinctive. What they call maize paper, a sort of dirty yellow."

"I thought it was the damp that turned the paper that colour!" Horrie said. "You know – damp tobacco making a stain —"

Crump said, "So *you* found it, Horrie?"

"Horrie found it," said Mr Pollitt. "By the barn. Very important clue. We missed it, Horrie found it."

"Why is it important?" Crump said.

"Because it's French. Couldn't be Frencher. You don't find anyone smoking those things over here, and a good thing too, they take the skin off your tongue and stain the paintwork. But in France. . ."

"Shanta's in France, then?" Jen said. "You agree with us?"

"There's *connections* with France, I'd agree to that," said Mr Pollitt.

"And telephone," said the sergeant, under his breath.

"What was that, Sergeant?" said Mr Pollitt.

"Speak up, man! Spit it out!"

"Telephone call," the sergeant said, unwillingly. "Didn't think you'd want it mentioned. All the same..."

Mr Pollitt frowned, drummed his fingers and at last said. "No point in keeping secrets from our young friends here. Shouldn't tell, but I will. You see, there's been a telephone call. Guess from where?"

"France," said the WCs.

"Right first time. From France. South of France. Call very garbled, didn't make proper sense, all very confused so far but we're working on it."

"The call was from a girl?" Horrie said. "Speaking English?"

Mr Pollitt nodded. "There you are then," he said. "Connections with France. French connections. You and your pendulums and funny feelings, we with our Official Channels. All pointing in the same direction. Oh – and Horrie's fag end. Smart work finding that. Important clue."

Horrie's grey face went a darker grey as he flushed with pleasure.

"France it is," said Mr Pollitt.

"Then why don't we do something?" Jen demanded. "Why not send someone? *We* know she's there, *you* know she's there – why not get *moving?*"

Mr Pollitt said nothing. They're right, he

thought. Right to be in a frantic hurry. But I can't tell them that...

And again... They're right, he thought. Right in thinking we're a lot of old PC Plods, sticking to the book, not getting on with it. They want to jump on a horse and ride off madly in all directions. And so, by God, do I. But I can't tell them that...

A telephone rang. He answered it, then said, "Got to go. Ask me where I'm going. No, don't bother. It's a meeting about your friend Shanta. Another meeting. There's nothing like meeting people, is there?" He left without looking back.

The WCs watched him go. "He's as fed up as we are," Crump said.

"He couldn't be," said Horrie.

"And here's me going off on *holiday*," Jen moaned. *"Tomorrow*. While poor Shanta..."

"That's right, you're off tomorrow," Horrie said, vaguely. "South of France. Lucky you." He picked at his lower lip.

"Cavalière," Jen said. "Just think, it's in the same part of France as Shanta! I feel so ashamed..."

Horrie suddenly and violently came to life. *"Tomorrow?"* he said. "South of France tomorrow? And you're going in that socking great mobile home of yours, I suppose?"

"Mobile *palace*!" Jen said. "We wave to the peasants as we go by. Ours is your genuine space-age jumbo vehicle. Real posh."

"How *big*?" Horrie said urgently.

"You've seen it. Gi-normous."

"Lots of rooms and closets and things?" said Horrie. Now his hand was on Jen's arm and his face pushed right up against hers.

"Lots of everything," Jen said. "What's on your mind?"

"Stowaways," said Horrie.

"What do you mean, stowaways?"

"What do I mean, stowaways?" Horrie mimicked. "Can't you guess? Even old Crump's guessed. Tell her, Crump!"

Crump, eyes wide with excitement, told her. "Him and me," he said. "Us. Hidden away. You take us to the South of France. When we get there, we just nip out and start walking. Towards Borme – and Shanta."

Now Crump, too, had seized Jen's arm and was staring urgently into her face. "What do you think, Jen?" he repeated.

Jen stared past the two urgent faces and with her free hand, carefully selected a strand of blonde hair and put it in her mouth. This told Crump and Horrie that she was thinking, hard. She chewed methodically for half a minute. She looked as if she had grown a blonde moustache.

"Well? *Well*?" Horrie said.

"Bikes," said Jen at last.

"Don't be stupid!" Horrie exploded. "It'd

take us days – weeks! – to get all that way on bikes!"

"I don't mean *that*," Jen said indistinctly through her moustache. She took the hair out of her mouth, looked disgustedly at the wet end and threw it behind her. "You'll need *bikes*," she explained. "I mean, you'll waste hours getting from Cavalière to Borme. Dad always takes folder-bikes. One each. Three bikes... Isn't that handy?"

"So you *will* help us to stow away?" said Crump.

"Of *course*! In the clothes closets. No trouble, unless Mummy suddenly gets all fashion-conscious. But no, wait, I'll arrange her clothes in the order she might want them."

"We'll have to leave our hiding places sometimes," Horrie said. "I mean, calls of nature and that."

"Wine bottles," Jen said, giggling. "And I'll let you out whenever I know it's safe. And see to your food and everything. It'll be fine, you'll see. We'll be in the South of France in two days. Daddy can't stand hanging around, he's always saying, 'Let's get there'."

"Hear, hear," said Horrie.

"Let's make a list of all the things we'll need as stowaways," said Crump.

Pollitt's Pension

The sergeant said, "Those Frenchies, the telephone people. They've been on again about an English-speaking girl."

"Girl got a name yet?" said Mr Pollitt.

"No, it's all still a mess. You see, the Frenchies contacted *our* phone people, and *they've* been in touch with Forensic, over here."

"But the call was made in the South of France? Definitely? There's no argument about that?" said Mr Pollitt. He was staring, working up one of his slow-burning, deep angers, the sergeant could see that. Because the wheels were turning too slowly. And there were too many wheels.

The sergeant said, "South of France. Definitely." Then he kept quiet and still, watching Mr Pollitt and wondering if there was to be an explosion.

However, when Mr Pollitt spoke, it was quite softly. "You're a well informed person," he said. "What's the quickest way to the South of France?"

"Don't know, Sir. And, Sir, you're in charge *here...*"

"Butterfly!" said Mr Pollitt. She had just entered the Incident Room. "You've been to France, am I right?"

"Yes, Sir. Three times. For holidays. It's

great!"

"Never mind that. You want to be there tomorrow, getting a lovely tan. How do you do it? Fly? Drive?"

"Well, flying, I suppose... No, there's too much sitting around in airports. A car. A fast car."

Again the sergeant saw Mr Pollitt staring. This time he stared at a big Police Rover, parked outside. He read Mr Pollitt's thoughts and said, "Look, Sir, you've got the Chief Constable at 1300 hours and a Progress Meeting at 1500 —"

"Meetings!" said Mr Pollitt. "I've had enough meetings for the moment, thank you very much. I fancy a relaxing little drive."

"But, Sir! That phone call – you can't go on that! – and besides —"

"Sergeant," said Mr Pollitt, "do you ever experience fuzziness, muzziness, that tired feeling?"

"But, Sir!"

"And you, Butterfly! Do WPCs ever go all vague and trembly and goodness-me-I-feel-so-strange?"

"Not me, Sir!"

"Oh yes, you do. Definitely yes. You too, Sergeant. Inefficient officers, both of you. Shocking memories. Can't even remember where your superior officer has gone."

"But, *Sir!*" said the Sergeant.

Mr Pollitt was at the door. He turned to say, "Got my passport, currency, luggage, all at the ready. There's efficiency for you! But you two — you're inefficient. And that's an order!"

Then he got into the Police Rover, revved the engine, slammed the door and was gone.

The sergeant said, "Well! What's all that about?"

Butterfly said, "It's obvious. He's been adding everything up, right down to pendulum and fag end. And he's said, 'To hell with this, I'm going to get that girl myself!'"

"But he can't do that, he's on orders here!"

"Of course he can't," Butterfly said. "And he hasn't as far as we know. Has he? Because we're inefficient, as from now. That's an order!"

"He's *barmy*," said the sergeant at last.

"Mebbe," said Butterfly.

"He's throwing away his career," said the sergeant.

"He's near retirement," said Butterfly.

"They'll stop his pension," said the sergeant.

"They won't stop him getting that girl home," said Butterfly.

"Well... I don't know..." said the sergeant.

"He does," said Butterfly.

The telephone rang. Butterfly answered it.

"It's for Mr Pollitt," she said over her shoulder to the sergeant. "You'd better take it."

She handed him the phone, looking into his eyes.

The telephone talked rapidly to the sergeant. The sergeant talked slowly to the telephone. "No, Sir," he said. "Haven't seen him this morning. No, he hasn't reported in. Oh, yes, Sir, as soon as he comes in. *If* he comes in."

He put down the telephone and gazed gloomily at Butterfly. "*None* of us will get our pensions," he said.

Stowaways

For the first few hours, Horrie and Crump quite enjoyed being stowaways. Jen, as she had promised, found them an excellent hiding place – a clothes closet in her parents' magnificent mobile home. The closet was high, wide and deep. Ideal.

The mobile home, envy of all eyes, glittered through London and Kent. Horrie's face was brushed by one of Jen's mother's silk-taffeta afternoon dresses. "Super pong," Horrie said. Jen's mother's taste in perfume was as expensive as her clothes.

Crump, framed in a two-piece on one side and a Paris-model disco outfit on the other, said, "Yeah, that's all very well, but it's getting a bit hot, isn't it?"

The miles rolled by. The stowaways got hotter.

Horrie tried pushing his selection of clothes along their hangers to make more breathing space for himself. "Do you *mind*?" Crump said, peevishly. In the dark of the closet, they began a silent, bitter fight: each tried to push clothes into the other's half of the closet. Neither could win. The clothes seemed to have an elasticity, a springiness. When you pushed them away they cunningly crept back again. Or they were pushed back by the other person in the closet, which came to the same thing.

Jen found an opportunity to slide open a closet door and see to the stowaways. "Gosh, your face is *purple*!" she told Crump.

"That's because we're suffocating," Horrie's voice told her from the darkness of the other side of the closet.

"You're *sweating*! Sweating all over Mummy's dresses!"

"The healthy perspiration of a noble British boy," Crump said. "She should be honoured."

"I don't think she will be," Jen said. "Oh, Lor..."

She slid the closet door the other way and revealed Horrie. He was not purple: more of a greyish mauve. His eyes were a rabbity pink. His face was glazed with sweat. "Warm for the time of year," he said, conversationally.

"Oh, Lor," Jen repeated, speaking with even deeper feeling. "I wish I'd *thought*..."

"*We* wish you had," Horrie said.

She hurriedly closed the closet door, not wishing to see anything more of the sweaty faces. "I'll have to find another place for you," she said. "Something's got to be done!"

At that moment, her mother came in. She had been sitting up front with her husband. Now she wanted a drink. "I thought I heard

117

voices," she said, eyeing her daughter with intelligent, determined, elaborately made-up blue eyes.

"Oh, no!" Jen said. "No!"

"But oh yes, yes!" said her mother, coming closer to Jen. "You said, 'Another place'! Then, 'Something's got to be done'!"

"Oh, that," said Jen. "That's the school play. It's called *Another Time, Another Place*."

"It's called *The Merchant of Venice* by William Shakespeare."

"Ah," said Jen, feebly.

"*Ah*," said her mother. Now her sharp eyes were roaming everywhere, taking in everything. Her friends said of her that she never missed a trick. Jen knew this to be a sound judgement.

"Something's going on," Jen's mother said as she expertly and rapidly made lemon tea in smoked glasses with chromium-plated holders. "You're hiding something."

"Oh, no, honestly!" Jen said. She had her fingers crossed behind her back. I'm not really lying, she told herself, I'm hiding *someone*, not *something*. Her mother's eyes were flicking in all directions, including the closet door.

"Oh, look!" Jen shouted. "The sea! I can see the sea! Oh, how exciting!" She pointed at the moving view framed in the mobile home's

118

windows: it was true, the sea was there, and perhaps Mummy would look at it.

Mummy did not. Mummy spoke. "Jennifer," she began (and it was always a bad sign when she spoke her daughter's name in full), "Jennifer, I'm not really in the mood for mysteries —"

Fortunately, she got no further. Horns were blaring, brakes screeching, and Jen's father was leaning out of the driving cab yelling, "*Tenez la gauche,* you lunatic!" to a French driver just off the ferry, who was driving on the wrong side of the road.

The mobile home lurched, tea spilled, slices of lemon took off and bounced on the floor and Jen's mother said a word she did not allow her daughter to speak. Jen let her breath go. For the moment, the crisis was over.

When the cross-Channel voyage was started and the mobile home was locked away on the car deck and the passengers explored the ship, it was safe for the boys to leave the closet and cool off. They gloomily sucked lemon slices and fanned themselves with fashion magazines.

Above them, Jen's mother ate potted shrimps in the ferry's best restaurant. "Something's going *on*," she said, eyeing her daughter suspiciously.

119

"Honestly, Mummy —"

"Your face is an odd colour. *Most* odd."

"It's the ship going up and down."

"You just ordered an enormous steak. And you wolfed down those prawns. You're not seasick."

"Yes, but I could *get* seasick."

Jen's father said, "In that case, I'll cancel the steak and save myself a lot of money."

"Oh, no, Daddy! Don't do that!" Jen cried.

The steak was important. She had ordered a big one because she intended to slice bits off, conceal them in her napkin and feed them to the stowaways.

This proved more difficult than she anticipated. Her mother kept glancing at her, sharply. Jen felt her face go pink, go white, and pink again as she conjured bits of steak into her lap. And the steak felt surprisingly hot against her thighs. It gave Jen a ghastly, guilty, glow.

When coffee came, she jumped to her feet, said, "I really do feel a bit queasy!" and ran off before anyone could stop her, clutching the warm parcel of steak. "But where can I *put* it?" she thought. "I can't get down to the car deck, it's locked up. And I can't carry it about with me..."

Eventually she had the bright idea of stuffing the steak between the plumply upholstered cushions of one of the many seats in a lounge. The lounge was almost empty, so it was easy.

But the lounge rapidly filled as people who had finished eating returned. Jen had not foreseen this. She reached for the steak – but it was too late: a nice, kind, friendly, fat woman bore down on Jen and said, "Oh, aren't I awful, but I *must* bother you! Because, you see, we were sitting here *before* and that's Ronnie's holdall to mark our place, and the newspapers too, you see there's seven of us and we'd got ourselves settled just where you're sitting, so *if* you could find another seat, I know it's a nuisance, but being *seven* of us..."

She beamed down at Jen. Behind her, six other faces, all fat and all smiling, assembled and beamed expectantly.

Jen panicked. "Oh, Lor!" she said – and almost ran from the lounge.

And that was the end of the stowaways' steak.

Butterfly, in the Incident Room, said to the sergeant, "Here's more about that phone call. The French one, from the girl who could be Shanta."

"Just come in, has it?" said the sergeant. He studied the report, then said, "Sounds like he's on the right track after all."

"You mean, Mr Pollitt? Of course he is. I

can *feel* he is. I just know it was our girl made that call."

The telephone rang. The sergeant answered it then covered the handset and muttered, "It's *them*, asking for *him* again." Butterfly pulled a face and shook her head, but the sergeant thrust the handset at her and said, "Your turn to be inefficient!"

So she lied into the phone till her face was bright pink.

The best but most expensive route to the South of France involves the longest Channel crossing. It takes you deeper south and avoids a lot of dull motoring. Jen's father, who never did things by halves, chose this way. So the crossing took hours and hours: and Horrie and Crump, locked away deep in the bowels of the ferry with empty cars all around them, became hungry.

"We can't eat their food," Horrie said. "Jen said her mother would notice. She notices everything."

"But I've got to eat," Crump said.

"You had lots to eat before we started, Jen saw to that. You can't be that hungry."

"I can. I am. All I can think of is food."

"Well, think of something else. Think what a happy little chappy you are to be out of the clothes closet."

"I'm not happy. I'm hungry. I wonder what

they've got in that fridge?"

"Come away from that fridge! Remember what Jen said!"

But Crump had opened the door of the neat, nice, fitted fridge. The interior light gleamed on jars, jugs, plates, platters, sausages, celery – everything you could want.

"Leave it alone," Horrie said. "Close the door."

Crump licked his lips and said, "This sausage thing in silver paper, she couldn't miss a slice or two of that, she could never tell we'd been at it —"

"Put it back. Seriously, Crump —"

"Wow, it's good! Sort of liver sausage, all thick and creamy, with bits and pieces mixed up in it! Frog sausage. They know their stuff, those frogs."

"Those bits and pieces are truffles. Cost a bomb. Put it *back*, leave it *alone*!"

"Have a bit of celery, Horrie."

"Don't! She'll notice! And leave those tomatoes alone!"

"You're right, I'll have a bit of cheese instead."

"Look, Crump, lay off! All right, I'll have just one tomato. The small one."

"And a bit of cheese to go with it. Open wide, there's a good Horrie. Down the little red lane, that's the way... Yum yum! Say, 'Thank you, Crump, that was ever so nice.'"

123

"Oh, belt up. And that's enough, close the fridge."

"Just one yogurt. We'll share it. I'll feed you with the spoon. Come on, now, open wide! The chuff-chuff's coming, where's the tunnel? Let's see that tunnel, Horrie. *Chuff* chuff chuff, whooo-*hoooo*!"

"Don't do that, it's running down my chin! Stop it, it's not funny!"

"*Chuff* chuff, chuff, whooo-*hoooo!*"

"Oh, that's just great, very clever, now you've got yogurt all over the carpet!"

It was the dark, damp stain on the carpet that gave the game away. Jen's mother saw it when the mobile home was zooming along the roads toward Dijon. The stowaways were of course back in their closet.

"Jennifer," she said. "Would you kindly explain this."

"Gosh, I don't know. Mummy, perhaps Daddy —"

"It was *you*, Jennifer. After making a fool of yourself over lunch on the ferry – pretending to be seasick, leaving perfectly good food on your plate and all that – you've been stealing food from the fridge."

"Honestly, Mummy —"

"*Jennifer*!"

"But honestly, Mummy —"

Starting a holiday abroad is always a tiring

124

business. Jennifer's mother had seen to the tickets and passports, packed everyone's bags, checked food and drink and bookings and a hundred other things. She was tired.

So tired that she slapped Jen's face.

It was an unusual thing for her to do, but she was tired and she did it.

The slap sounded very loud and the silence that followed, very silent. The stowaways heard it. They also heard Jen gasp; and the sound of her crying.

Though Horrie and Crump liked to think of themselves as hardened ruffians, neither could stand seeing or hearing Jen (or Shanta) suffering. When a WC, boy or girl, cried, it was a serious matter that had to be attended to.

So the doors of the clothes closet slithered open and first Horrie, then Crump, stepped out into the open.

"What's up?" Crump demanded fiercely.

"Are you all right, Jen?" Horrie said ferociously.

Both glared at Jen's mother with pink, puffy eyes in sweating, purplish faces (the closet had become hotter than ever). Crump's hair stood up in damp tufts. Horrie's was a sweat-darkened, hideous mop. They looked ridiculous but determined.

Jen's mother looked back at them with a determination that had nothing ridiculous about it. "What the *hell*," she said, coldly and clearly, "are you two doing here?"

The mobile home was directed smoothly into a lay-by; Jen's mother and father stood confronting the WCs; and there had to be explanations.

At the end of the explanations, which took a long time, Jen's mother looked silently at her husband and said, "Are you thinking what I'm thinking?"

Jen's father, large, horsy, competent and always in control, said, "I hope so."

Jen's mother tapped a varnished fingernail on a Formica tabletop and said, "We're on the same side, then?"

Jen's father said, "If you mean *their* side, yes."

Then Jen's mother, who had only recently slapped Jen's face, reached across to Jen and gave her a brisk kiss.

Jen started crying, but also laughing. Horrie and Crump looked at each other, baffled.

Jen's father said to them, "Right. We've got to get moving!" He went to the driver's seat, started the motor, and the mobile home surged away on its journey to the south.

"It's OK!" Jen explained to Horrie and Crump. "It's all arranged! Mummy and Daddy are taking us straight there! Taking us to Shanta!"

"Well," Horrie muttered, "taking us in that general direction, anyhow."

"We hope," said Crump.

French Fry

Though her left foot trailed a red mark with every step, Shanta kept running. She had trodden on a sharp rock, a thorn, a piece of glass – whatever it was, the pain of the wound stabbed at her, and sticky red blood clogged thickly between her toes.

The wound stabbed: her throat was being sandpapered. Each breath was a rasping agony. The air was filled with smoke and fire, with cinders and hot dust. She could hear her own breath, a ridiculous noise, a dry, gritty mooing.

Ahead of her, the woman ran. She was like a grotesque bundle on legs. The bundle of household possessions rolled and swayed; under it, the woman's dark, bent, leathery legs buckled and pumped. Her right hand clutched at the bundle. The left held a battered doll. The little girl held the other arm of the doll, which linked the two figures together.

It was a strong doll. It had to be. For the little girl kept stumbling, even falling. She used the doll to pull herself to her feet. She ran and fell, ran and fell.

Shanta saw the child fall yet again. This time she did not get up. Now she was like a doll herself, with her legs stretched out in front of her, her mouth a perfect O, her star-like hands reaching towards the retreating figure of her mother. Shanta realized that the mother did not know the child was left behind.

The little girl raised her head to the burning sky and screamed. The mother was now too far ahead to hear. Shanta stopped running. She stared, appalled, at the child – at her mop of black hair, jerking and bobbing in time with her screams; at the blood on the torn knees; and at a little brown foot, twisted inwards. Oh no! Shanta thought, Oh no, no, no – her ankle's gone!

Shanta tried to scream for help but her throat was raw. She wanted the boys to help carry the little girl. But the boys were nowhere, anywhere. They had long ago thrown away their burdens and bounded about like mountain goats. And, already, the mother was almost hidden in rolling clouds of smoke.

"It's got to be *me*," Shanta sobbed. "I've got to do it. It's not *fair*."

She lifted the child. At once the little girl's arms and legs went round her neck and chest like clamps and her shrieking mouth was right against Shanta's ear. "Don't *do* that, be *quiet*!" Shanta tried to tell her, but her throat only croaked.

Shanta gulped down burning air and broke into a shambling run, staggering under the weight of the little girl. "Other side, other side!" she cursed – for the child was on her left side, weighing down on her left foot, the foot that hurt so much. She tried to swing the child round her body but the arms and legs tightened their grip each time; it was impossible.

Endlessly on. After a time, the panting screams the child made in Shanta's ear sorted themselves out. It was not the child after all, it was a pop group she was hearing. In a disco. Lots of lights, and that smoke stuff, what's the name, carbon dioxide, dry ice. The smoke stuff choked her, so Shanta switched programmes and brought in Julie Andrews.

"The hills are alive... With the sound of muuu-sic!" Julie sang. Funny joke, ho-ho. The hills were definitely alive, Shanta was on a hill and it was alive. It had to be alive because it kept biting her left foot: its sharp teeth bit, clawed and stabbed. You're in pain, real pain! Shanta congratulated herself. You're experiencing genuine agony!

She knew what to do about it. You just kept on running, the pain could not keep up. And now she had a police siren to clear the way for her, a siren that shrieked and whooped like a little girl. Or was it a disco?

Suddenly things went wrong. She was too good a runner, that was the trouble, her legs were running away from her, she could not keep up with them! Come back, legs, wait for me! But they wouldn't, they began to slither and slip, stumble and trip, they were going, gone...

She went down like a skyscraper falling. It seemed to take minutes for her to hit the ground. At last the ground came up – SLAM! – and then there was darkness.

A face came down on Shanta like a helicopter landing. Oh, hello, thought Shanta, you're the gypsy woman in the place Mr Brasen called India, but it's not India, it's France. Why am I lying on the ground? Why are you bending over me? Why are you touching my face with your dirty fingers? Your fingers are dirty with blood! *My blood!*

Shanta tried to sit up but the woman held her down. Now the woman was talking to her, pumping words at her in French. Shanta thought, Miss Loomis will be very pleased with me for understanding so much. The woman kept saying, *Bonne, tu es bonne.* That means she thinks I'm good. *Tu as sauvé ma petite:* I have saved her little one – the little girl. *Courageuse*! So I'm brave. Whoopee.

Now the woman was kissing her hand, big wet kisses. This action so disgusted Shanta that she sat up, violently. Sitting up cleared her head. Suddenly the nightmare was gone, everything was real again. She was at the foot of a steep, rocky hill; so steep that her legs must have run away with her as she rushed down it, clutching the child.

And there was the little girl, her ankle bandaged, sitting staring at her bloodied knees, touching the blood. Her head was cut too. And her elbows.

Blood: what about me? thought Shanta. Her left foot hurt so much that it did not matter any more. The pain was hopeless, incurable, it would never get better. The woman was working on her foot, dabbing at it with the edge of her skirt, squawking over it like a sympathetic hen.

Shanta began coughing. The sky was a swirling horror of red, brown, grey and black: from it rained hot dust and ashes, and the little black or gold curlicues of burned or burning vegetation. The boys stood staring at it, tensely. The woman shouted, "*Allez, allez!*" She tried to pull Shanta to her feet. The boys joined in, tugging at her. Shanta did not want to get up. She wanted to lie back and die.

They would not let her die, they kept dragging her on, wrenching at her arms, lifting her when she fell. Shanta remembered Jen taking a toss from her pony at a gymkhana, and everyone crowding round to help, but Jen's mother kept hooting, "It's *per*fectly all right, *hon*estly, *per*fectly all right..." That was what Shanta wanted to tell the woman and the two boys. But they got her to her feet all the same.

At last, the five of them formed a sort of crab, a body linked by arms and extending legs in all directions. This crab staggered down the hill, spinning feebly, losing and regaining legs.

The crab collapsed inside a sudden oasis of coolness. There was a cave, a small, rocky retreat: the fiery air rushed past the mouth of the cave, sucking coolness from the huge rocks. The five of them collapsed in the dimness, gasping and sobbing with exhaustion.

The woman was the first to recover. She was on her hands and knees, with her head hanging down. Like an animal, Shanta thought. And, like an animal, the mother hung over her youngest child, cooing hoarsely at it, wiping its brow, touching the cloth wrapped round the twisted ankle. Shanta would not have been surprised if the woman started licking her offspring.

Now the mother once again turned her attention to Shanta – "*Comme tu es courageuse, comme tu es brave!*" Shanta thought of Miss Loomis's ladylike French-speaking voice and compared it with the woman's. Different as chalk and cheese, she thought. What is the French for cheese? *Fromage.* She could not think of the French for chalk. Not that it mattered. Nothing mattered, except the

133

coolness of the cave.

The older boy was on his feet. "*Eh*! *Eh*!" he said urgently; then a string of words Shanta could not understand. But it was easy to understand his gestures. He was pointing outside to the swirling red and brown sky – to the flecks of fire that danced and whirled – to tumbling black balls of smoke rushing over the ground, rolling backwards instead of forwards, confused by the hot blast that drove them on. "*Allez, allez, allez*!" the boy shouted.

Shanta did not want to *allez*. "I've had enough!" she said, peevishly. "Leave me to *die*, I'll be a French *fry*!"

She thought this rhyme very clever, very funny, she wanted to tell it to everyone. But now the woman was at her again, explaining and acting out a complicated message. Shanta at last understood it. The woman meant, "You are our prisoner. We cannot let you go, because we are afraid of Mr Brasen. But we could let you *escape* – that would be quite different! But please, if ever you meet Mr Brasen, do not give us away! You *escaped*, remember!"

"OK," Shanta said wearily. "Anything you wish. *Comme vous voulez. D'accord.* Can I go now?"

The woman squawked, the boys argued – and they were on the move again, running, lurching, tripping. The bigger boy seemed to know the way. He led them through the searing wind, the raging, burning atmosphere. The little girl clung to Shanta's hand. Shanta wished she wouldn't. The mother kept throwing admiring, doting, sideways glances at Shanta. Shanta was past caring.

Then peace again as they ran round and under a great pile of rocks. The flaming wind howled past this little mountain, leaving only small whirlwinds of brown dust flecked with twisting black ashes. Again the five of them could stop, collapse and groan.

"*Là!*" squawked the woman. She pointed to a stone cottage. Shanta stared at it in amazement.

The cottage was real, proper, civilized! There was a garden with a real red watering can! And a clothes line with a real aluminium prop! And curtains in the windows! And a sun-lounger chair with wheels!

True, the roof of the cottage was smoking and the sun-lounger's bright cover was dotted with black, smouldering holes — but the cottage was real and the woman was saying it was hers, Shanta's!

Shanta gaped at this beautiful, civilized cottage, then smiled at it possessively. She hardly felt the woman's hands clasping her own, or bothered to respond when the woman held up the little girl to be kissed goodbye. She did not hear the words of gratitude the woman poured out – the same old stuff about you have saved my little one, you are truly a saint! She wanted only to be left alone to enjoy the delights of the cottage. Under its friendly roof there must be a bedroom: and in the bedroom, a *bed*.

Still squawking gratitude, the woman at last backed away. The boys scowled and twitched. They wanted to get on. They could see a clear road to the sea and safety.

Shanta stood watching them limp and stumble into the distance, wishing the woman would not keep turning to wave to her – for Shanta had to crack her dry mouth into a smile and wave back each time. But at last, they were gone.

At last she was alone.

At last she could go to bed, bed, bed, bed; beautiful, beautiful *bed*.

"Latest from France," Butterfly said, handing the sergeant a printout. "Looks pretty definite, wouldn't you say? It *was* Shanta."

"Voice-prints and everything..." said the sergeant. "Cor, isn't science wonderful? I suppose they matched bits of their recordings to scraps of cassette from a school play, or something." He re-read the printout. "Hardly any doubt now," he said. "That telephone call from the South of France *was* Shanta. So

136

the chief was right."

"Everyone was right, all along," Butterfly said. "The kids, Mr Pollitt – everyone!"

"I'll give you odds he'll still lose his pension," said the sergeant, gloomily.

Damn Foreigners (1)

"Damn foreigners," Mr Pollitt said. He was lost again.

The main part of the trip had been easy. His "borrowed" Police Rover gulped the French autoroutes so fast that he had to keep turning over his folded map to keep pace with his progress. But now the easy part of the journey was over. He was in the true South, the rocky, strangely scented, twisting-and-turning South. The heat was getting to him; his forehead prickled, the sun glared, the distances seemed all wrong. The signposts named unexpected places.

Worst of all, nobody spoke English. Mr Pollitt had memorized the few words he needed – the French words for, "Excuse me", "Which is the way to", "Say that again, if you please", "Many thanks". What he had not foreseen was, that the French would *reply* to his words. They replied in French – grunts of French that made no sense; or torrents of French that made even less sense.

So yet again, Mr Pollitt pulled off the road and studied the map. When he reached his destination, he was to look out for Emergency Centres. That was obvious. The trouble was, getting to his destination. His head ached so badly that the map seemed to glare at him, then go out of focus. The prickling of his forehead was now beads of sweat and the sweat got into his eyes. He swore, got back on the road and drove on.

He knew he was on target when he smelled fire and saw smoke. But then, he knew that he was not going to get there when uniformed figures, arms raised, barred his way, stopped his car and asked questions in a language he could not understand. He showed his police identification: no good. He said, "*Je cherche... je cherche une fille ... très important, savvy?*" – but they wouldn't savvy, they just talked and shrugged and stood in front of the Rover.

Now the sweat really poured down his face. He was on to a loser and he was not used to losing.

Damn foreigners.

Damn Foreigners (2)

The mobile home had a diesel engine the size of a large truck's. Its chassis was rather longer than that of a London bus. It had eight wheels with great thick tyres that never punctured. It was a marvellous machine, fast, secure, impressive, enviable. If you saw it, you would think, Wow, they must be rich.

Its only fault was that it was a devil to reverse.

In summer, the South of France is jam-packed with people and vehicles. The roads leading to the coast are mostly scenic, small, curly and hewn out of rock. Many people are terrified of these roads: often they snake through places with sheer rock on one side and sheer drops on the other. Only the shining, silvery guard-rails edging the roads give the faint-hearted motorist some slight hope of staying alive. "I wish I could drive nearer the centre of the road!" this driver says — "but of course I can't, there are cars and trucks hurtling at me from the opposite direction, and there's another corkscrew corner coming, and that red car's blaring its horn at me..."

So the nervous driver's hands get sticky on the steering wheel and the guard-rails seem to come closer and closer to the side of his car, threatening to tear off the door panels.

Jen's father was not like that. He drove his superior machine as if he himself were a machine. Before every hairpin bend, he sounded the mobile home's brazen horn. If the cars did not get out of his way at the sound of that horn, they very soon did when they saw the mobile home coming towards them. It was huge. It gleamed and flashed. And it was driven by a big, broad-shouldered man who obviously knew his business.

So – rapidly, smoothly – Jen's father piloted the great vehicle along the most direct path to Borme.

"Only an hour or so to go," said Jen's mother. As she spoke, she gripped the arms of her chair (they were going through yet another hairpin bend).

"Only another hour," Crump replied. He grinned. So did Horrie. They too had to cling to their seats.

Then there was a massive screeching, tearing sound and they were all lying on the floor of the mobile home.

When they got to their feet and sorted themselves out, they saw that things were not as bad as they had sounded. A small, old Renault had got itself entangled with a new Audi saloon. Already everyone had left the two cars. They stood waving documents at each other, talking very loudly in French. No one was hurt and the cars had suffered only minor harm.

Almost at once, the French police were on the scene. They arrived on BMW motorbikes. The machines and men had a super-efficient, superhuman look. But the men turned out to be only too human after all...

For when they had finished taking details of the Renault, the Audi and their occupants, which took a long time, they started talking in short, nasty sentences to Jen's mother (the only one who spoke French).

"I don't believe this!" she told her husband, after a minute's conversation. "They're trying to make out that we had something to do with the accident!"

"Oh, for heaven's sake! Explain!"

She explained. The mouths under the helmets and visors grew tighter; the police notebooks no longer waved – they jabbed, accusingly. Then, worse still, the French people from the two cars joined in. They waved their hands, talked all at once and began to enjoy themselves.

"Oh, Lord. I get it now!" Jen's mother muttered. "It's one of those 'Them and Us' situations. Oh Lord, Oh Lord..."

Horrie did not understand. Crump did. "Don't you see," he explained, "they want someone else to blame - *us*! Because we're English and they're French ... and worse still, we're in this socking great mobile palace

142

and they're just in ordinary cars. So we're the villains, we've *got* to be!"

"But that's crazy!" Jen said.

"But true," Jen's mother said over her shoulder.

"It's all going on too long," Crump said. He was squirming with anxiety to get back on the road, the road to Shanta.

"They're telling us to move our vehicle! To back up!" Jen's mother said. Now she too was squirming; but with anger and frustration.

"Tell them not to be fools," Jen's father said grimly.

"You must!' said the policeman, in French.

"We won't!" said Jen's father, in English.

At last, though there was no point in reversing the mobile home, he had to give in. Fuming, he sat in the driver's seat and engaged reverse. Sweating, he fed the power through. The mobile home shuddered and juddered, and would not move.

Swearing, he did what he should have done in the first place: he released the handbrake. Its power suddenly unleashed, the mobile home bucked and jumped backwards. Its vast rear bumper instantly flattened the whole front of a Peugeot saloon with six people in it, all French.

Jen had to shout to make Crump hear above the din of furious voices. "Bikes!" she

143

yelled. "*Bikes*!"

Unnoticed, they clambered up the metal ladder leading to the roof of the mobile home. Unheard, they tried to tell Jen's mother what they were up to. Unseen, the three of them, Jen, Horrie and Crump, pedalled off along the curling road that shimmered with heat, making their way to Shanta.

The Call

Shanta found the bed.

She had already opened the little fridge, drunk some orange juice and eaten a dried-up corner of cheese. The cottage's occupants must have taken everything else with them.

She soon knew a lot about the occupants. They were a Danish couple – there were Danish paperbacks and a Danish-flag paperweight. They were young: the clothes they had left were young people's clothes. One or both was a photographer. There were transparencies and prints everywhere, even fanned out in front of the sofa. The photographs had a professional look.

Upstairs she found the bed. It was a double bed with a patchwork coverlet. By it there was an opened bottle of white wine and two tall glasses. She filled a glass and sipped wine, staring at the bed. She was almost crying with pleasure. *My bed! For me! I will lie on you and sleep for ever and ever!*

To tease herself by delaying the glorious moment, she went down the stairs for another look at the living room of her magical cottage. She sipped the wine. It was too warm. Well, everything was too warm because of the great fire. She took another sip, feeling the warm wine spread warmly inside her. Everything was warm, even the cottage's walls. Was the cottage on fire? Probably. Did it matter? No.

She looked out of the window. To her left, smoke and fire: to her right, a silver, glittering band. That was the sea, the cool sea. She would make for the sea when she had quite finished sleeping in the beautiful bed.

She sipped wine from the tall glass. The sun-lounger outside caught her eye. It was pock-marked with black holes. Some of the holes released tufts of smoke. As she watched, a red-hot cinder fell from the sky and burned itself into the cover of the sun-lounger. It burrowed in, then smoke came out. Interesting! Another sip of wine. *Oh, goody gum drops, I'm getting tiddly. Time for bed, beautiful bed! Just flop down on it, dried blood and all. Sleep.*

More wine.

She limped up the wooden stairs. They seemed to sway. The wine. But no, they really were swaying! They were coming away from the wall! Impossible!

Then the roof and one wall fell in and the stairs collapsed and Shanta fell down with them, still clasping the wine glass.

At first she could only think one thought: *no bed.* It was a dreadful thought. It made her cry. Then she noticed that the roof timbers tumbled all round her were smoking and hot to the touch. Of course! The burning roof had fallen in. She saw little flames come from some blackened timbers and peevishly threw all that was left of her glass of wine over them. As this had no effect, she threw the glass as well and giggled spitefully to see it break.

"But this is serious," she told herself, out loud. She stood up and her brain whizzed round in her skull. "Tired, terribly tired," she said out loud, soulfully. "Tired and bashed about and *no bed*. And the cottage is on fire." She was surprised at how little all this bad news affected her. Her head was muzzy, her mind was gone, she felt like giggling – but suddenly burst into tears instead.

The tears seemed to wash her mind. All at once, she knew exactly what to do. She had to telephone Mum and Dad. The phone call would solve everything. Simple.

She looked for the phone. She knew she had seen it somewhere, earlier on. Over there, in that corner, on a little table. Ah, there it was: red telephone. But now it was under a pile of smouldering timber. The pile radiated heat. She went to the kitchen for the oven gloves she had noticed earlier, paddy-paw gloves connected to each other by a band of fabric. It was awkward putting them on and it felt funny wearing them. Animal paws. She clapped her hands together, pawed at the air and said, "Miaow! Miaow!" Being a pussy cat started her giggling again.

She pushed and shoved at the timber. Some of it was crinkled, black and smoking – almost alight. Most of it was just very hot. There was dust everywhere and the dust was hot too.

She cleared enough timber to reach the telephone and pulled it towards her on its coiled cord. It was a funny telephone. It was all wobbly. It looked like a telephone made of Plasticine, a melting telephone, a dribble-droopy telephone. She realized that this was because of the heat. The poor thing was half-baked! Ho, ho, funny joke. But the dial still spun, so she dialled her home number, holding the hot, misshapen handset close to her ear. While she waited for Mum or Dad to answer, she picked at the scabs on her knees and frowned. Even her knees were spinning round, they were as bad as the walls and everything else. All that wine.

It was a stupid telephone. It would not answer her. It just made high-pitched telephone noises and, sometimes, burrs and beeps and crackles. She shook the handset crossly and shouted, "Mum! Mum! It's me! Shanta!" It did no good, so she dialled again.

The phone made the same stupid noises as before so she answered the noises just as stupidly. "Miaow!" she said, as loudly as her sore throat would let her. "Miaow, Miaow!"

Just as she was getting really good at cat noises, a voice from the phone interrupted her.

"*Allo!*" it said. "*Allo – allo!*" Then it said several more things, all in French.

"This is *me*," Shanta said, loudly and importantly. "I want to speak to my *mother*. It is *most urgent*."

"*Allo!*" said the telephone. "*Tenez ... Allo! ... Répétez... Qui est là? Allo, allo! Parlez, parlez!*"

"My mother," Shanta said. "I want my *mother*."

"*Parlez!*" said the telephone. It was getting excited and urgent. "*Dites-moi votre numéro! Vous êtes Anglaise? Oui?* Geeve ... mee ... your ... number. Geeve mee your name, your address!"

"Never mind all that! I want my mother!" Shanta begged the phone. "Please! My mother!" Now she was sorry for herself. The room spun, one of her scabs had started bleeding, she was never going to sleep in that bed. She looked wildly at the photographs spread on the floor. None of them showed Horrie, or Jen, or Crump, or her parents. All strangers. "Give me my *mother!*" she howled.

But the phone would not listen. Now the first voice had gone away and there was another female voice, speaking better English.

149

"Where are you?" it demanded.

"In the fire," Shanta said. "There's a big fire... I'm in it. Everything's foreign. Let me speak to Mum or Dad, they'll understand!"

The phone went on being stupid. Instead of letting Shanta talk to her parents, it kept asking where she was — what was the number on the telephone — even what she could see from the windows of the cottage. It was confusing. So was the sound of her own voice. Her throat was so sore that it sounded like someone else's.

Beyond everything, the phone seemed to be lonely. It kept begging Shanta not to go away, not to hang up, to keep talking. This began to get on Shanta's nerves. Once or twice she answered, "Miaow!" when the phone asked a particularly silly question — but she did not let the phone hear her cat noises, that would have been rude.

"Your name, your address!" the phone asked, for the umpteenth time. Shanta lost patience with it.

Spitefully and deliberately she put the handset back on its cradle, with her little finger daintily crooked to show her scorn. Then she left the cottage. "Why stay?" she asked herself. "I mean the bed's gone and the place is on fire anyhow. I think I'll be ill and find a hospital. Hospitals have beds."

She started walking. Her leg felt a bit bet-

150

ter. Or was that the effect of the wine?

The phone kept quacking away to itself for quite a long time after she was gone.

That was the call that the French telephonist had conscientiously reported to her superiors – who had reported to British Telecom – who had contacted the police – who had analysed, dissected and probed every syllable – and had concluded, "It must be Shanta."

That was the call that had been the last straw that broke the camel's back, as far as Mr Pollitt was concerned; and sent half a dozen people on the same mission to the same destination: France.

Everything Wrong

Mr Brasen said, in his usual mixture of bad French and bad-tempered English, "*Quoi? What?* *Ecoutez*, moron, I pay you plenty — *beaucoup d'argent* — to deliver the goods. I don't want excuses."

The swarthy man he spoke to replied, in his usual mixture of gypsy French and bad English, "*Si, si.* OK for you, Monsieur, but there is this *orage du feu, effroyable*; this fire storm, Very bad, *horrifique*. Make everything bad, *difficile, impossible.*" He gave a huge shrug.

"But Ricardo, *où est-il?* He's supposed to be here today — *ici, aujourd'hui*, with the goods! He's supposed to deliver! But now *vous dites il est perdu*: you cannot find him." Ricardo was a carrier, one of the men who brought drugs to the distribution centre.

"*Oui, perdu*, no find him." Another huge shrug. "*Peut-être il est mort.* The fire. Many people dead."

"But he's got the goods, he's got to be here, the boat is waiting."

"*Ah, le bateau, le bateau . . .*" This time, the swarthy man did not shrug. He made a whistling grimace and sucked in air between two discoloured front teeth. Mr Brasen knew exactly what this gesture meant: confusion, mess, things going wrong, trouble.

The swarthy man showed the yellows of his eyes and began talking fast and persuasively about money. He needed money, Mr Brasen owed him money, it was not his fault that the region was on fire, that the goods could not be delivered, perhaps everything would come right if Mr Brasen gave him so-many thousand francs.

"*Fermez votre boîte!*" Mr Brasen exploded, in his best and worst French. The words mean "Belt up".

Mr Brasen turned his back on the swarthy man, hunched his shoulders, and thought. Everything was going wrong. The great fire had prevented the swarthy man from bringing his contribution to a major consignment. The failure of even one carrier was dangerous; bad.

Worse, there was the problem of the boat. The boat waited offshore for the consignment of drugs. The drugs, packaged in very small loads, should, at this moment, be finding their various ways to the boat. The boat would take them to a ship in Marseilles – and so to a world full of sickness and suffering, which Mr Brasen's drugs would profitably increase.

But the drugs were not here; the boat was most probably cruising aimlessly up and down the coast, its captain sweating with fear. The boat was an expensive-looking launch, a rich man's toy. Mr Brasen used such a boat because the rich were expected to behave unreasonably – to drift up and down a coast, for example; or to anchor for an hour or a day or a week with no apparent purpose.

But Mr Brasen had used this boat too many times, perhaps. It was quite possible that it had attracted official attention. Perhaps even now powerful lenses were looking at it, and official brains were wondering why there were no pretty girls stretched on its idle decks, why no jovial men poured drinks in tall glasses, why its captain cut such a grimy, worried figure.

And anyhow, where *was* the boat? And its cargo? Mr Brasen did not know. Nobody knew.

He bit his thumb and surveyed the crowded beach. Hundreds, thousands, of heads and bodies faced the blue sea. But one young man, deeply tanned, stood with his hands on his hips looking inland, towards the balcony of Mr Brasen's villa. His whole body seemed to ask a question.

Mr Brasen knew this man – and what the question was: *When?* When do I collect that bright plastic picnic box from your villa – the box packed tight with the drugs that should have been delivered to me by Ricardo? When do I walk down the beach with the box, perhaps holding it aloft for my girlfriend to see? And when does she smile and wave as if

154

to say, "Ah, good, now we can go and have our romantic meal on the water, bobbing about in your grey and yellow inflatable with its flashy, king-size outboard motor"? And when, instead of having that meal, will I be able to zoom out to the waiting launch, and hand over that "picnic" box? And when will I have earned my pay packet, my many thousands of francs? *When*, Mr Brasen?

Mr Brasen swore and turned his back on the beach and the handsome young man.

The swarthy man standing before him grinned and writhed his body ingratiatingly. He meant, Just a few thousand, perhaps, to go on with?

"*Pas d'argent*," said Mr Brasen. "Not a cent. Find Ricardo – deliver my stuff – then plenty *argent*, right? Until then – *rien*. Nix. *Comprenez*?"

The swarthy man gave one of his smaller shrugs, coolly swallowed a drink Mr Brasen had poured for himself earlier, and prepared to leave. At the doorway, he turned and smiled at Mr Brasen. The smile was like a dose of snake venom. "Oh, get out!" said Mr Brasen.

The man got out. Mr Brasen bit his thumb. He had no answers to any of his problems. He needed a drink.

He picked up a glass. It felt sticky. It was the glass the swarthy man had drunk from. A fly buzzed round it. Mr Brasen pulled a face and went for another glass. The fly followed his sticky finger.

It was a fat, juicy, disgusting fly. Mr Brasen was in the mood to kill something: the fly would do. He seized the garish local newspaper and swatted at the fly. He missed. He tried again and missed again.

Furiously, he threw the newspaper at the fly. The newspaper flew open and its pages spread themselves all over the floor. Brasen swore and kicked at the newspaper – then froze, knelt on the ground and began reading.

JEUNE FILLE ANGLO-INDIENNE, said the headline. "Young English/Indian girl." The girl had been found that morning wandering through the burned-out countryside. She had been taken to an Emergency Centre at a place only forty kilometres away.

It could be Shanta. Surely it could only be Shanta?

He had to know. He had to be sure. If it was *not* Shanta, he could continue to breathe and sleep. If it *was* Shanta, something would have to be done. Something violent and final.

His BMW glinted in the sun outside his villa. Within a minute, Mr Brasen was at the wheel, pointing the car north – away from the sea, towards the fire. And Shanta.

The Chase

Mr Brasen was a good driver. The BMW was a good car. But for once in his life, Mr Brasen drove badly – recklessly – dangerously.

Everything was against him. The roads twisted and corkscrewed. Their broken verges sent shocks through the steering wheel to his too-tense hands. And soon, the fire itself turned against him. Smoke darkened the view. Human figures suddenly emerged from the smoke, waving their arms at him, trying to turn him back.

A group of police scattered as the BMW rocketed through.

The policemen were not having this. Three of them flung themselves into their big Citröen and took off in pursuit. Mr Brasen gritted his teeth, snap-changed down to third and left black marks on the road. In his mirror, he saw the police car rock and dig in on the bends. Mr Brasen knew how to drive fast but so did this police driver.

He should not have looked in the mirror – for suddenly, right in front of him, there was a van with a TV camera and cameraman on top. The van was crawling, Mr Brasen was touching seventy. He jerked at the steering wheel and screeched into a flat, sideways skid. He missed the van and hit rock with one of his rear wheels. The BMW bounced back on course. He was safe. Lucky.

Or was he? Now the car steered badly, there was a sort of wambling, squirming feeling from the back end. And in his driving mirror, he glimpsed the Citröen, snaking smoothly along the curling road, its roof light twinkling officiously, its headlamps glaring through the smoke.

Mr Brasen snarled and put his foot down. The BMW's engine purred throatily. But the rear end of the car felt like a farm cart on a ploughed field.

Mr Brasen fell into a rhythm of swearing – a rhythm broken when he came across a cluster of vehicles and people, even some tents. A field hospital, an Emergency Centre, that was what it was. He had to slow. People were waving angry hands and fists at him. He changed down to second, clamped down on the horn and bulled his way through.

Now the police Citröen was closer than ever.

Smoke got in his lungs, sweat in his eyes, and his brain pounded. Perhaps Shanta was in that field hospital? Perhaps he should already have found her and was in the process of losing her! But there was nothing he could do. The police Citröen was behind him and steeper, rockier, smokier hills ahead of him. He could only keep on.

Mr Brasen knew the worst when the BMW started making noises like a steel band. "Rang-a-dang," it went. "Rangle-dangle-rang-a-dang." He had time to guess what it was: a rear wheel was coming off, probably complete with its half-shaft. He had time to clench his teeth, correct the beginning of a wild slide, then correct the correction by spinning the steering wheel to opposite lock.

But that was all he had time for. All at once the BMW went crazy. It lifted its rear, tilted, screeched and went into a howling, yelling skid that gouged hot tarmac off the road.

Through the windscreen, the last things he saw were sloping blurs of road, rock – and then, impossibly, as the BMW rolled, the sky.

The first roll flattened the roof and spewed broken glass.

The second flung one front wheel, the rear axle and boot lid into the path of the Citröen.

The third ended in a hideous, long-drawn-out, metallic crashing and crunching as the car beat itself to pieces along a wall of harsh rocks.

The police Citröen weaved through the wreckage and halted. The BMW was right way up. The three policemen took their time getting out: they had seen all this before along the sun-drenched roads of that glorious coast – young morons doing impossible speeds in sports cars, smashed-up fat cars full of

159

smashed-up fat people; every kind of motoring fatality.

"*Dommage*," one policeman muttered as he reached through the shattered window and switched off the BMW's ignition. "*Dommage*,"... a pity. He was referring to the car. He admired BMWs.

Another policeman began talking into his pocket radio, ordering an ambulance. "No, not dead. Not yet, anyhow. Yes, everything necessary..." He shrugged and helped attend to Mr Brasen. Everything necessary. They disconnected the battery, tore off the driver's door, cut away the seat belt, checked for petrol leakage, propped open Mr Brasen's blood-soaked mouth, made sure he was able to breathe – everything necessary.

Quite soon, an ambulance arrived and the stretcher carrying Mr Brasen was manhandled into it. The policemen kicked the worst of the rubbish left by the crash off the road; shrugged their shoulders; smoked a quick cigarette; and radioed in. "Resuming normal duties."

The French doctor in the field hospital shook his head as he examined the new patient. This one would die. No point in moving him to the hospital in town: too many question marks about internal injuries.

Patiently, the doctor got to work on Mr Brasen, beginning at the beginning and working his way through. But the man would die.

To his amazement, the dying man suddenly opened his eyes and even tried to sit up. "Where's the boat?" he yelled. "Where's Ricardo? We've got to get the stuff out to the boat!" Then he fell back, unconscious.

"Phew!" said the doctor to his two nurses. "We've got a tough one here! What was he saying?"

"He was speaking English," said one of the nurses, "that's all I know."

"Well," said the doctor, "I'd better keep trying. What antibiotics have we here? What drugs?"

The senior nurse told him. The doctor frowned. "I'll need more than that," he said. "Radio Medical Centre. Say I want the stuff fast."

He began dictating the list of medical supplies he would need to treat this extraordinary patient, this amazingly tough Englishman.

Frizz

"After this one, the English girl," the nurse reminded the doctor.

"Ah, yes. Her. *La Mystérieuse*."

They called her *la Mystérieuse* because she had appeared from nowhere, limping on bloodstained feet and legs; and knew nothing about herself. She had lost her memory. "But she can still come in useful to translate," the nurse had pointed out.

Their extraordinary patient, the Englishman who refused to die, was still trying to talk through his broken teeth. "The boat ... get the stuff to the boat..." he would say; and many other meaningless things, all in English. The doctor sank a needle into the man's arm. Soon the talking would stop.

"All right, the girl next," said the doctor. "Wouldn't it be nice if, just for once, we had a patient who spoke French?" He smiled and shrugged.

They entered the tent where Shanta lay – or should have been lying. In fact, she was on her feet and twisting her hair about. *"Comment ça va?"* said the doctor. "OK, yes?"

"OK, *oui*!" Shanta told the doctor and the nurse. *"Vraiment* OK."

The doctor looked into her eyes. They flickered. They worried him. He told Shanta to follow the ballpoint he moved from side to side in front of her. Shanta obeyed uneasily: her head ached, she did not want to look at the ballpoint. "My eyes are OK," she said. "Look!"

She squinted horribly at the doctor. "Do not be ... chee-kee!" he said, laughing. He liked this girl. She had been knocked about; perhaps she was even suffering from mild concussion; but she was getting better by the minute. She still coughed a lot because of the smoke, but that would cure itself. Her lungs were undamaged. The cuts and swellings on her legs, elbows and hands were unimportant, there were no broken bones underneath. Her memory would return in time.

The only thing that really seemed to trouble her was her hair; it was singed and frizzy. She kept touching the burned ends.

"You think you are ... verree *laide*, uglee?" the doctor said.

"You're no oil-painting yourself," she replied, grinning.

"*Quoi*?" said the doctor. The nurse couldn't understand either, so they shrugged, laughed and prepared to move on.

"*L'Anglais*," the nurse reminded the doctor. "The Englishman."

"*Ah, oui*. We have an English man," the doctor told Shanta. "A patient. *Il ne parle pas Français* ... You help us *comprendre*, yes?

Traduire – translate his words for us?"

"Yes, OK," Shanta said. "*Traduire* OK."
She was interested. She needed something to
do. "*Maintenant* – now?" she asked.

"*Non, non* . . . We make him to sleep. *Mais,
bientôt.*"

"Yes, soon. Soon as you like. Whenever
you say."

They left. Shanta, alone again, sat on her
bed and stared at the canvas walls. She
wished she had a mirror. She knew her hair
was a mess. Still, there was the Englishman to
look forward to.

She did not think of her parents; or her
friends; or of home and England. She had
forgotten all about them. Her mind had been
wiped clean, like a tape.

All she was clear about was that her name
was Charlotte, or Sheila – something beginning with a Ch or a Sh; and that she did
not like fire. When they had carried her into
this place, one of the men carrying her
stretcher had lit a cigarette. Shanta had
started screaming, trying to escape, trying to
hit the man.

She hated fire and smoke. She did not ask
herself why.

She felt no curiosity about herself and her
past. She did not ask herself how she came to
be where she was. Nothing worried her. If
you lose your memory, you cannot remember

what to be worried about. Getting her hair right – that was the important thing. She fingered the uneven, frizzy ends and thought, You idiot, why didn't you ask the doctor for a mirror?

That was all she needed – a mirror.

Puncture

"Stop!" Jen croaked. "I think I've got – oh, hell, I *have* got..."

"A puncture," Horrie said. He and Crump wearily got off their bikes and bent over Jen's rear wheel.

Crump pinched the flabby tyre. "Just what we needed," he said thickly. "Great."

Jen was wailing, almost crying. Horrie was swearing, dimly. Crump lifted the rear wheel and spun it, trying to find the cause of the puncture. "I don't know why I'm doing this," he suddenly burst out. "I mean, it isn't as if we had a repair kit." He picked up the bike and flung it on to the rocky verge. "Now what do we do?" he groaned, and threw himself down beside the useless bike.

Jen began crying in earnest.

Horrie said, "I just don't care any more," and threw himself down beside Crump.

Sweat poured down scarlet faces. Passing cars flung grey and yellow dust that clogged the sweat.

Jen put her head between her knees and howled steadily. Crump tiredly reached out to stroke her back and drearily chanted, "*There*, Jen, *good* Jen, not your *fault*, Jen, come *on*, Jen, *smile*, Jen."

Horrie crooned, "All over now, Jen, *there's*

a brave girl."

After a time, these childhood chantings got through to her. She stopped crying and even laughed, shakily. "But we're finished, we've failed," she complained. "I mean, there's nothing left for us to *do*."

"Still got the old pendulum," Horrie said. He pulled it from a pocket and swung it about on its string.

"Pity we haven't got a map to go with it," Crump said, disgustedly.

"I'll draw one," Horrie said. He began scratching in the thick dust with his fingertip. "There's the sea," he said. "And here's the hills behind us. And here's the road. Now, come on, pendulum: *swing*."

"Oh, belt up," Crump said, not angrily. He knew that Horrie was as exhausted as himself. He felt sorry for both of them, all three of them. He watched the pendulum through eyes that stung with sweat. It just swung in vague circles.

"Stop a car, get a lift," Jen said. "That's what we must do!" She stood up and looked determined.

"A lift to where?" Crump said.

"To where Shanta is!"

"Where's that?" He said nothing and sat down.

Horrie went on swinging his pendulum. The sun beat down. The hot air scraped their lungs. Passing traffic thickened the coating of dust over their sweat.

They must have looked as pathetic as they felt, for a passing Renault Espace – a "tall car", a sort of mobile living room in which you could sleep – miraculously slowed, stopped and backed up to them; and an English voice called, "You all right?"

"No!" cried Jen, Crump and Horrie, all together.

The miracles continued. The Renault belonged to a young doctor and his lady friend. They came from somewhere near Newcastle. The lady friend kept telling the WCs exactly where the place was. She had a high-pitched voice, all on one note, and said, "Yerss" at the end of her sentences.

"Oh, it's a lovely district when you get to know it, yerss, and the cultural amenities are surprising, really they are, yerss."

The young doctor said nothing. He just frowned and drove. It was easy to see that the two of them were not having a successful holiday. Probably the doctor had been glad of the interruption caused by the three WCs and their bikes, which littered the back of the smart Renault. "Well," the lady friend had said, "I *suppose* you can put them there ... yerss." Then she started gabbling about the place near Newcastle.

Just when the WCs were beginning to itch and twitch with anxiety about getting a word in edgeways, the final miracle occurred. It took the form of a *bleep* and crackling noises.

The doctor took a small handset hidden in his jacket pocket and said, "*Oui?*" to the handset. Then, "*Oui, je comprends*," and switched off. Over his shoulder he told the WCs, "Useful gadget. Glad I brought it. They're expecting us. I think it's about fifteen kilometres to the Centre —"

"Centre? What sort of Centre?" Jen and Crump said, both at once. "Emergency Medical Centre. I tuned in to it on this radio gadget. I'm a doctor, they need doctors. So —"

"Shanta could be there!" Jen shouted.

"Who or what is Shanta?" the doctor said.

The WCs explained. He listened. The lady friend said, "Yerss." The Renault kept rolling on towards the Medical Centre.

And, perhaps, Shanta.

They went along blistering roads flanked with rocks that radiated waves of burned air; through ginger clouds flecked with black wisps; past groups of men flailing at living flames that refused to die.

And all at once, they were there, at the Centre, and the doctor was being told not to stop here, not to park there, but ah! you are a medical!, then over there if you please. There were vehicles all over the place, Army, Police, medical, tourists' cars and mobile homes, fire engines – even, glittering in the distance, what Horrie thought to be a Police Rover from England. But that was impossible.

Then he glimpsed something even more impossible – Shanta! Shanta, a long way away, almost hidden by lots of hurrying figures – but Shanta! It wasn't really Shanta, of course; for this dark, slim girl was staring at him but through him. And anyhow, her hair was wrong.

Then some Frenchmen pushed and pulled at him, they wanted to set up TV stuff where he was standing. When he looked again, the girl who resembled Shanta had gone.

Square Smile

The doctor said, "OK, now you visit him. But he is *très malade*, very ill. We desire you should understand who he is, and what he wants. He is ... *troublé*, you understand? In the head." He twiddled his forefinger against his temple. "He *wants* something very bad," the doctor said. "To cure him, it is necessary that we understand..." He ran out of words and shrugged his shoulders.

Shanta said, "I'll try and find out what is worrying him. OK? Perhaps he knows he is allergic to certain medicines."

"Yes, yes, it may be that. Now I must go."

He hurried off.

Shanta walked forward into the dim brown of the tent, towards the bump on the bed that was an Englishman. Or an Egyptian mummy. White pillow, a head bound in white bandages, two black holes for nostrils. The square slot of a mouth.

Square. The mouth was square.

Shanta stared at it and her mind jerked backwards, into the past, showing flashes of places and things, echoes of sounds and voices. It showed her her own bedroom with the Mickey Mouse alarm clock on the bedside table. Suddenly, very loud in her ear, her mother's voice said, "Oh, you are so bad, your room is a *mess!*" "But, Mum, I'm doing my homework..."

Then the whirring tapes of her mind stopped dead. Her fingers moved over her face, feeling it. This must be me. What is Me? And that on the bed, that is an Englishman. What does that really *mean?*

Never mind. She had to deal with him. The man with a square mouth.

She crept closer to the man. He seemed too still, too neatly arranged, to be human. The lips of the square mouth were parted and moist. The bedclothes rose and fell slightly as the lungs pumped noisy breath.

Her knee brushed against a chair by the bed. On the chair there was a bowl with a syringe in it. Syringes are for medicine, Shanta said to herself. The syringe rattled. The man on the bed breathed in sharply.

Then his eyes were wide open, staring at her.

His eyes had to roll sideways to look at her. His neck, she saw, was locked in a surgical collar. One arm was hidden in the bed, the other, in plaster, lay on the blankets. The fingers of this arm moved. Then his lips.

"Dark girl!" he said. "*Got you!*"

His fingers scrabbled like spiders' legs: the white plaster arm shuffled across the rough

172

blanket towards her. The sound, faint as it was, put her teeth on edge. She pulled away from him, her teeth bared and her mind jangling with blurred memories, all of them hateful.

The fingers drew the heavy white arm to the rounded edge of the bed. Then the arm slipped, with a jerk.

"Hurts!" he grated. "Help me!"

She shuddered. Beneath the cast there were broken bones, torn flesh. What agony he must be feeling! She could see little of his face because of all the bandages. But she saw sweat beads jump out under his eyes and a sort of yellowing around his nostrils.

"*Hurts...!*" the square mouth gasped.

With infinite gentleness, she took the spider fingers of the broken hand. She must do nothing sudden, everything softly. She must return the hand and arm to its former position so that it would no longer hurt. Yet slow and gentle as she was, each tiny movement of the heavy arm cost the man agony. Shanta's eyes brimmed with tears. The square mouth writhed, the tongue showed between the broken teeth. "I'll be gentle, very gentle," Shanta promised.

"*Murdering pig,*" her mouth said.

Shanta did not hear it speak. Patiently and tenderly, millimetre by millimetre, she moved the arm.

Outside and above her, there came the blattering sound of a helicopter. The noise became louder and louder. The canvas walls of the tent flapped and bulged. Then the noise died down and she could hear excited French voices, sounding pleased. She thought, Of course, the helicopter is bringing in medical supplies. To save people's lives.

Suddenly, the man was staring straight into her eyes. At first his look was animal: it could only mean "stop it hurting, make me better." The look in his eyes changed and took on meaning. "The stuff," he muttered urgently. "We've got to move it, you know? That fool Ricardo..."

She concentrated on the arm. She was succeeding, she was moving it, soon the poor man would feel less pain.

"*Pig*," her mouth said. "*Foul, filthy pig.*"

"If it weren't for Ricardo, I'd have a hundred and fifty thousand clear," said the square mouth. "And a million in Marseilles. A million – just waiting!"

Now the arm was where it should be. Shanta leaned back, wiped the tears of sympathy that blurred her eyes, then closed them. She would rest, just for a minute.

But she could not rest! – the Primus needed pumping, if it wasn't pumped straight away WCHQ would be filled with smoke and smuts and Jen would moan and worse still the tea wouldn't get made! Her eyes opened wide with the shock!

But it was all wrong, there was no WCHQ, no Primus; only this tent and the man like an Egyptian mummy. Again her hands went to her face, feeling it, trying to know it.

The nurse hurried in, brisk as a robin, carrying a stainless-steel dish containing a little bowl filled with cottonwool, syringes, hypodermic needles and some neat little packs.

"Chopper is arrived, yes?" she said, waving her free hand to imitate a helicopter's rotor.

"Yes, chopper," Shanta said. "I heard it."

"It is arrived from Marseilles, it brings many things we need!" said the nurse. She pointed at the stainless-steel dish. "*Bon*," she said.

"*Bon*," Shanta agreed. Syringes, needles, cottonwool – and those neat little packs. She had seen them before. These very packs. Where had she seen them before?

Packs. Drugs.

Packs. Drugs.

The nurse leaned over the Englishman. "He say things to you?" she asked Shanta.

"What?"

"He say things? Tell you things?"

"No, nothing," Shanta said. She was staring at the little packs; or staring through

175

them. Poor child, thought the nurse, she has been through a lot. But quite soon she will be herself again.

"He's very sick, isn't he? Terribly sick," Shanta said.

"*Quoi?*" said the nurse.

"He is not looking good," Shanta explained. "Not good at all."

But the nurse was doing business-like things with her syringes, needles and neat little packs. "You go now," she told Shanta. She smiled and said, "*Allez, allez, allez!*"

Shanta walked slowly to the flap of the tent, then turned and once again stared with see-nothing eyes. "*Allez!*" the nurse said. "*Et merci bien!*"

Shanta walked away, very slowly. Englishman. Square mouth. WCHQ. Packs. Drugs. The Englishman was ill, very ill, not good at all. Not at all good.

Unknown to her, her mouth said, "*Filthy murdering pig.*"

A man strode towards her, a big gawky man with an overheated face. He was wearing the wrong sort of clothes, no wonder he was so hot. Shanta moved aside to let him pass, but the man stood in front of her, he put his bony hands on her shoulders.

"Shanta!" he said.

"Let me go." She struggled, but there was

no strength in her. And anyhow, it had all happened before. Soon this man would throw her in the back of a lorry that went *Yerrk!* when it changed gear, but she'd escape into some woods. And after that —

"Shanta!" the man repeated. "I've got it right, haven't I? Course I have. You're Shanta."

"Don't touch me," Shanta said. She was afraid he'd grab hold of her hair, her hair was a mess. She needed a mirror.

He was shaking her shoulders, not hard, it did not hurt. "You've *got* to be Shanta!" the man said. You could see the skull under his face. Yet it was quite a nice face. He lifted her chin with a hard finger and stared at her. "You *are* Shanta!" he said. "Definitely. Thank God. Poor kid."

"I've got to go now," Shanta said. There was something about injections, packs of drugs. The packages held tiny little doll's-house bottles. But these had rubbery caps, you pushed the needle through the cap and drew out the contents of the bottle into the syringe. Next, you wiped the patient's skin with surgical spirit on cottonwool and then – Ugh! They told you you'd hardly feel it. After, they said, "*What* a brave girl!"

No, that wasn't right. It was the Englishman in the tent, *he* was to have an injection. Drugs. Packs. The lorry. Something wrong.

"Come with me!" the man said. He had her arm, he was pulling her along. He would take her back to the cave with the woman who shouted, "Cur faytew dank". Shanta didn't want any more of that, thank you. The man pulled, she pulled against him. It became a tug of war. Shanta began yelling. People turned to look, lots of people. They stared and shouted foreign things, there was quite a crowd. Shanta did not mind. She was a WC, the other WCs would come and rescue her in the nick of time – then back to WCHQ, out with the Primus, all have tea.

And suddenly they really were there, all three of them, running through the crowd, flinging themselves at her, hugging and kissing her! Darling Jen and beautiful ugly Horrie and Crump like a mad gnome with tears squirting out of his crinkled-up eyes! All around her, all over her! And this is our friend Mr Pollitt, he got to you first, *we* wanted to be first, it's not fair, but who cares, oh Shanta, we've found you, we've missed you so much...

The tapes in Shanta's mind jerked backwards – forwards – then, suddenly finding their proper places, slithered with perfect evenness and smoothness through her mind.

Yet still there was something wrong, terribly wrong. Shanta's tapes glided through her mind: the stories they told at last made a

178

sequence, at last made sense. "Quick! Come with me!" she shouted. Now she was dragging Mr Pollitt's arm, rushing him towards the tent and the Englishman who was not good at all – towards the little packs of drugs with the sickeningly familiar labels – towards the doll's-house bottles filled with doses of pain and death...

The nurse looked up, surprised, from Mr Brasen's bedside. "*Eh, alors!*" she began, but was overwhelmed.

Only Jen could make herself understood in French. "Have you used these on anyone *else*?" she cried, holding a little bottle in front of the nurse's nose.

"*Non* – we are so busy – *mais bientôt,* when there is time..."

The Egyptian-mummy figure on the bed groaned and stirred. Mr Pollitt gazed at it, expressionlessly, for some time. "Dose of your own medicine," he muttered. Nobody heard him.

Heavenly Choir

Double-you see...aitch kew,
How I ....love yew!

Shanta sang, loudly and repetitively.

"Oh, do belt up!" Horrie said. "I can't stand you when you're cheerful!"

"But I'm happy! I'm home, and it's all over, and I'm back in WCHQ. *Double-you see ...aitch kew.*"

"Look, belt up or we'll get you kidnapped again," Crump said.

Jen said, "Make some tea, or something, Shanta. Anything you like. Just don't sing."

"You can't stop me being happy," Shanta said, giving everyone saintly smiles. "I mean, here we all are, and we can't be chucked out because Mr Brasen isn't here to chuck us out... Wait a minute, I made tea last time, it's Horrie's turn!"

"Wow, this place pongs," Horrie said, gloomily. "Hot weather doesn't suit our stately home. All the old rat droppings warm up, I suppose. Begin to ferment."

"I think it's terrific," Shanta said. "I think it's the best place in the world!"

Horrie drew water from the tap. The trickling water was browner and smellier than ever. Crump began to light the old pump-up stove. The smell of meths and hot paraffin tried to drown the animal and vegetable smells of the barn, but failed.

"Bet you he'll be back," Jen said.

"Who?" said Crump.

"Brasen, of course. He'll have survived. Bet you anything you like. I can just see him now, looming up ... first his rotten shadow, then *him*, filling the doorway."

"Don't drivel," Horrie said. "He's breathing his last in France. Cor, you're right, Jen, it was like that, wasn't it? – the day he came here to chuck us out, I mean. First there was his shadow —"

"Look!" Shanta said, her voice a hollow whisper. "Look outside!"

They looked. Outside, in the brightness, there was a long shadow. The shadow of a man.

The shadow moved, lengthened, came nearer. The figure of a man was silhouetted blackly in the doorway.

"Mr Brasen!" Shanta said, and shrank back.

"Mr Pollitt!" Jen said – and ran forward to throw her arms around him.

"Enough of that," he said. "You don't treat senior police officers like that. I'm thirsty. Any tea? If young Master Crump doesn't pump that stove, the meths will burn away."

"Pump, Crump!" Shanta said. "Jolly joke, ho, ho!"

Crump pumped. The stove spurted a ring of blue flame, and hissed cosily. The WCs sat Mr Pollitt on a crate. Jen stood behind him with an arm round his neck. She said, "Your sunburn's fading. You might even go brown."

"Pigs might fly," said Mr Pollitt.

Crump made tea. Nobody seemed able to think of anything to say. Everyone's mind was turning over rapidly, thinking thoughts.

Jen was the first to speak. "What about *him*? Mr Brasen?"

"Ah," said Mr Pollitt. "Got some bad news for you, I'm afraid."

"You mean, he's still alive?" Horrie said.

"Tck, tck," said Mr Pollitt. "No, on the contrary, he has passed on. Gone before. Joined the Heavenly Choir. Found eternal rest."

"Kicked the bucket?"

"That was what I was trying to imply," Mr Pollitt said.

"Tough," Horrie said cheerfully.

"*Quel dommage*," Jen said, in her best French. "Too sad."

"Do you think it hurt much?" Crump said hopefully. "Lots of groaning and screaming and threshing about?"

"Sure I don't know," Mr Pollitt said. "But now let's drop the subject. A sensitive lot like you, it'll all end in tears. Look, that tea will be stewed if you don't pour it. If it's agreeable, I'll have mine in a *clean* mug."

"A clean mug?" Jen said. "You must be joking."

Mr Pollitt took his hot, sweet tea and sipped it. "You lot," he said. "You'll never reach old age. Muck like this in mugs like this... You'll poison yourselves."

The word "poison" stuck like a burr. Mr Pollitt, knowing he had said something wrong, coughed, got to his feet and strolled out of the barn. He wondered who would follow him. Someone would.

It was Horrie. He said, "What was the *cause* of death? What was the Coroner's verdict, or however they do it in France?"

"I don't speak French," said Mr Pollitt. "No comprenny. And you don't either. Least said, soonest mended. Stop worrying."

"It's not me I'm worrying about," Horrie said. "It's Shanta. She talked an awful lot over there in France. And there were all those reporters listening."

"There always are," Mr Pollitt said.

"I heard one reporter say, 'It'll be interesting if that man dies.' And another reporter said, 'You mean, because of the girl?' And the first reporter said, 'Yes, she's just spilled the beans about the dud-drugs racket, yet she *allowed* that Brasen fellow to be pumped full of dud drugs.' Then the *second* reporter said, 'Well, he isn't dead yet.' And the *first* reporter said, 'But if he does die, there'll be quite a story to be told about the girl allowing the drugs to be used.'"

"You're such a worrier," Mr Pollitt said. "Lad your age – you ought to be playing conkers or something."

"No, seriously," Horrie said.

"All right, then: seriously. Shanta didn't *allow* your friend Brasen to be pumped full of anything. She'd lost her memory. Didn't find it till she met up again with you lot."

"You know that and I know that," Horrie said. "But suppose someone told the story a different way?"

"Shanta's a minor and I'm a recently promoted police officer. Can't prosecute her, can't argue with me. Forget it."

"So Shanta's all right?" Horrie said.

"Shanta's always been all right," said Mr Pollitt. "She was born that way. Mr Brasen wasn't. Anything to add to that?"

"Suppose not," said Horrie. "It's been weighing on my mind, that's all. Shanta's had enough. I'm glad you think she'll be left alone." He took a deep breath and grinned. They walked back to the barn together.

It was noisy in the barn. Shanta's hair was being styled. Her arms were locked behind her by Crump so that Jen was free to do the styling. It took the form of tufts and spikes. There was a plait with a teaspoon woven into it. Crump found a worm and offered it to Jen. "Plait that in too," he said. "It will give a sense of *movement*, don't you think?" Shanta struggled and howled, half laughing, half angry.

"Dear oh dear," said Mr Pollitt. "Breach of the peace." He refilled his mug and went outside again with Horrie. Horrie said, "What did you mean, 'recently promoted'?"

"What? Oh, that. Yes, I've been moved a step up the ladder. I thought I'd get the chop for pinching the Rover and acting on my initiative, but no. Now I'm flavour of the month."

Butterfly drove up in a police car and said, "Mr Pollitt! They're yelling for you at Division. I've got to drive you there straight away."

"Time to be off," said Mr Pollitt. He did not hurry to the car. He said, "Yes, flavour of the month. Most Popular Policeman. Because alone and single-handed, I smashed an international drugs ring and rescued a damsel in distress. Definitely."

Horrie's face fell. "I like that! We helped! We did a lot!"

"Not the way I tell it," Mr Pollitt said, smugly. Then he saw Horrie's face, stopped walking, and said, "Ah, come on, now. Just joking."

"Better hurry, Mr Pollitt," Butterfly said,

trying to get him into the car. But then Shanta, Crump and Jen roared out of the barn, all shouting at him.

Mr Pollitt stared above the WCs heads and said, "Listen, you lot. I have something to say. You did a *good job*. You did all right. Got that? Good. Now I'm off."

He folded his long legs and big feet into the car. Jen shouted, "You're coming back? We'll see you again?"

"Oh, yes. Someone's got to keep an eye on you," Mr Pollitt said menacingly. "I'll be back. Definitely. With handcuffs."

The car started. Mr Pollitt scowled at the WCs. They waved and cheered. Jen started to cry. When Crump scornfully asked her why, she hooted, "I *like* crying."

"I like tea," Crump said. "Come on. Let's brew up again."

Inside WCHQ, the old Primus spurted flame under a kettle filled with brackish water. The flames dimly lit the faces of the four WCs.

Crump said, "Go easy with the tea leaves, we're running short."

Jen said, "I wasn't really *crying*. Just a mild weep-up."

Horrie said, "Give me the comb, Shan, I'll do the bits you can't reach."

Shanta said, "It's awful, it's terrible, it'll never come right." She was still half cross, half giggling.

Outside, the light faded over the fields. Deep in the soil, the worms went about their business undisturbed by flutes, vibrating garden forks, steel rods, the Vibro Miracle or anything else.

THE TIME TREE
Enid Richemont

Rachel and Joanna are best friends and the tall tree in the park is their special place. It's Anne's too. So it hardly seems surprising that the three girls meet up there – except for the fact that four centuries divide their lives.

"Ms Richemont develops her story beautifully, with finely controlled writing and clear delineation of her three main characters." *The Junior Bookshelf*

IN BETWEEN TIMES
Hannah Cole

At first, it's boring for Karen at Mrs Cholsey's, the child minders's, where Dad makes her go before and after school. But then Stacey starts going too – and the two of them can stand together against the hostile and superior Timothy Cholsey. And that's when, for all three children, the real adventures begin...

"A brisk, wrly humorous narrative." *Chris Powling, TES*

"Hannah Cole skilfully links three stories... Exciting reading." *The Guardian*

PIG IN THE MIDDLE

Sam Llewellyn

When 11-year-old Alec Whean rescues and befriends a stranded seal pup, he soon finds himself in the middle of a furious struggle between the "green" Blue People and a savage, seal-hating local fisherman. To save his new pal Alec needs to take drastic and daring action. But will his strength and courage hold up?

"Exciting ... this absorbing book is very hard to put down... The ending is surprising and generous." *The Sunday Times*

MORE WALKER PAPERBACKS

For You to Enjoy

☐ 0-7445-1333-2   *The Arpino Assignment*   £2.50
                     by Geoffrey Trease

☐ 0-7445-0847-9   *The Horn of Mortal Danger*   £2.50
                     by Lawrence Leonard

☐ 0-7445-1431-2   *In Between Times*   £2.50
                     by Hannah Cole

☐ 0-7445-1420-7   *Pig in the Middle*   £2.50
                     by Sam Llewellyn

☐ 0-7445-1355-3   *The Fire of the Kings*   £2.50
                     by Julian Atterton

☐ 0-7445-1447-9   *The Time Tree*   £2.50
                     by Enid Richemont

☐ 0-7445-1399-5   *The Water Cat*   £2.50
                     by Theresa Tomlinson

Walker Paperbacks are available from most booksellers. They are also available by post: just tick the titles you want, fill in the form below and send it to Walker Books Ltd, PO Box 11, Falmouth, Cornwall TR10 9EN.

Please send a cheque or postal order and allow the following for postage and packing:
UK, BFPO and Eire – 50p for first book, plus 10p for
each additional book to a maximum charge of £2.00.
Overseas Customers – £1.25 for first book,
plus 25p per copy for each additional book.
Prices are correct at time of going to press, but are subject to change without notice.

Name _____

Address _____

_____

_____